CH00943516

Five Wee

A story of courage and resilience during the summer
months of 1940.

Inspired by real events.

Graham Strachan

Dedicated to those who served in the Royal Naval Patrol Service (1939-1946).

Preface

The Crux of the War

25th September 1940, Harwich

Summer unfolds slowly, as the country comes to terms with the first anniversary of the outbreak of war. Nerves are tested, as people swap rumours of the enemy's invasion plans and try to imagine the horrors that will follow. Bombs are cascading down on London as the Blitz takes hold and families seek shelter in Underground stations to avoid the physical and mental scarring caused by the destruction of their homes and workplaces.

Stories of extreme courage reach the public as young men dice with enemy aircraft over the skies of England as the Battle of Britain defines the final line of resistance in this year of determination. People have been tested over the past year, especially by the events of May when the phoney war gave way to the humiliation of Dunkirk. On that occasion feelings of desperation were recovered by the resourcefulness and bravery of the small ships of Operation Dynamo, as they worked hard to save the British Army.

As tensions surface again, everyone is harbouring dark thoughts. The public stop short of sharing these doubts beyond the closest of family, but everywhere there is a collective and unspoken sense of fear. Fortitude becomes a way of life as the military's actions fuel the nation with their acts of selfless bravery.

Hidden away from people's attention are many lesser-known contributors to the defence of the nation. The English Channel and the North Sea are part of the supply chain routes that keep the country stocked in a range of items, from everyday necessities to the vital tools of war. The protection of these shipping lanes is entrusted to a remarkable and resolute group of minesweepers and converted trawlers. This collection of ships is manned and operated by the Royal Naval Patrol Service. In complete contrast to the might of the Royal Navy, these small ships are crewed by men with an irreverent attitude to military ways, but who stand brave and steadfast in their resolve to protect Britain. These men are given the nickname Churchill's Pirates.

The RNPS Pirates are men drawn from various pre-war occupations and their introduction to naval operations is both rapid and all-encompassing. For over a year, men connected with the sea have been volunteering and travelling from ports across the country to help build the RNPS at its Lowestoft headquarters, fondly referred to as the Sparrow's Nest. In some cases, the RNPS has attracted men to join their ranks from the Royal Navy, and the Royal Naval Reserve, as they clamour to see early action. Rapid growth in men and ships transforms the

Sparrow's Nest into a fully-fledged naval shore base, called HMS Europa, and from this station, Royal Navy command and control structures direct the protection of the Channel and North Sea. As dangers grow, the RNPS responds.

The Port of London is the largest commercial port in the world, and it operates at the heart of the country's supply of goods and machinery. Large cargo ships fight their way through raging storms, and the perils of the Battle of the Atlantic, to reach Britain's western and northern ports. From there, smaller ships transfer the goods and travel along the east coast, forming a vital artery to supply London. These coastal convoys face a constant threat from the enemy, as they come under attack along the whole length of their journey. As an island nation, Britain must rely on its seaborne routes for survival.

In the summer months following Dunkirk, the RNPS builds on its involvement in the rescue efforts by expanding its coastal protection role to focus on the threat of Nazi invasion. Enemy mine-laying operations fill the sea with their deadly cargo and the Kriegsmarine's fast E-Boats control the waters along the coasts of occupied countries. Hitler is planning his invasion, code-named Operation Sealion, to first gain air superiority over the defenders, before mounting a full-scale land invasion. Raging through the clear summer skies, the Battle of Britain dominates the minds of so many, as the country watches the Luftwaffe attempt to destroy the RAF and clear away this brave line of defence. Eventually, a wayward enemy bombing raid on London causes Churchill to respond by bombing Berlin, and as a result, Hitler changes his strategy. These actions intensify to bring about attacks on London's homes, factories, and docks, culminating in the Blitz. The diversion of enemy bombers away from Britain's airfields allows the RAF to recover and rebuild.

Warfare in the Channel and North Sea escalates, causing damage, loss, and destruction. Despite the many demands made on the staff of the RNPS, all matters of safety must be investigated by a dedicated team of officers, as lessons need to be learnt and corrective action taken. This is the story of one such investigation.

On the morning of 25th September 1940, Commander Wilkes from HMS Badger is setting up a Board of Enquiry in the administration building that once operated as the Great Eastern Hotel. Wilkes contemplated his return from an enjoyable retirement after spending many years of meritorious service in the Royal Navy. He thought long and hard about re-joining but concluded that he was well suited to a role upholding the best customs of the senior service. Specifically, he volunteered to return to investigate incidents falling under HMS Badger's command, helping to disentangle the reasons behind the increasing number of incidents involving the ships of the RNPS. His no-nonsense approach will bring clarity at a difficult time.

Commander Wilkes returns a salute and greets the Lieutenant who is sitting on the Board of Enquiry and who is tasked with making the arrangements and administrating the session. 'Good morning, Dickerson.'

'Good morning, Sir', replies the Lieutenant as he hands the Commander a file containing the papers for the enquiry. Noticing the perfect turn out of the older sailor, the lieutenant knows he is in the presence of a fastidious man and realises that everything about the enquiry will be by the book.

'Ah, good. I see we have all the signal reports we requested,' says the Commander with some relief.

'Yes, Sir. We have all the details collated. It was a tight deadline to meet,' replies the Lieutenant before showing the Commander towards the enquiry room.

'Yes, it's not easy investigating an event that happened just three nights ago. Well done Dickerson,' concludes the Commander as he opens the door and enters a room already filled with naval staff and witnesses.

Commander Wilkes prepares himself and waits for the room to settle as he checks the name on the front page of the enquiry paperwork and wonders how this terrible incident came about.

Chapter 1

Ties to The Sea

20th July 1940, Pembroke Dock, West Wales

Memories of the winter's extreme sub-zero temperatures have faded, as warm sunshine now lifts all but the hardest of hearts. Fresh reminders of the war's threats are everywhere, especially with the recent news that the enemy has landed on British soil and is now occupying the Channel Islands. People throughout the country are hungry for news as the Battle of Britain rages above and leaders from both sides reach new heights of wartime rhetoric. Test

Robert lives in Pembroke Dock, a small town sitting in a commanding position on the Milford Haven waterway. This large natural harbour in West Wales has always provided a home to ships and has supported several military roles during its history. Getting its name from the neighbouring medieval town of Pembroke and the establishment of a Royal Dockyard in 1814, the town sits on a site with direct access to the south of the haven. With the waterway and the sea beyond, the town grew around the might of the dockyard and using the best of Victorian engineering, a defensive fort and two Martello towers were built to provide protection.

Built on a ridgeway, the town's gentle slopes are laid out in a regimented pattern of streets that run down to the edge of the waterway. The growth of the town peaked during the second half of the nineteenth century and Robert now lives in one of the large Victorian houses originally built for the senior dockyard staff. The house sits towards the top of the town, on Victoria Road, a street that takes its name from the Queen whose navy constructed most of the area. The military heritage of the town may serve it well in the immediate months to come.

Sitting at the breakfast table, Robert drinks his strong tea, and while looking at the large hands clasping his mug, he sees skin engraved with a record of hard work and years of cruel weather. At the age of thirty-one, he feels young and positive, but remaining seated he ponders the future with some concern. 'What a time to raise such a young family,' he thinks, as he focuses on the war correspondent's stories contained in his newspaper. Normally, he would devour the news reports, searching for any indication of how the war is unfolding, but his mind is wandering. Relaxing at home and enjoying his Saturday morning breakfast is one of his treasured times, but not today, not while he has a difficult decision to make, not while his mind is churning through his options.

Robert is a serious person who spends time thinking through the details of his life. A strong disposition and hard years at sea make him appear older than his true age, but he presents a trustworthy and reliable face, enhanced by clear blue eyes that relax those in his presence. He is proud of his Scottish roots and people warm to his soft lyrical accent. Many consider him a gentleman in all senses of the word.

Wanting to be smart and well-presented when not at sea, his appearance is enhanced by a clean-shaven face and light brown hair, kept short with a strong parting on his right side. There are signs of his hairline receding, but outdoors that is nearly always hidden underneath one of his natty caps. His features are well proportioned and in a smart suit, you would not detect his incredible strength. Indeed, many consider him as a slight man with not an ounce of excess flesh on his frame, but the truth is he is a product of his strong genes and a tough living.

Being one of nine children, he has learnt to support those around him. He does not tolerate selfish behaviour and always tried to support his mother and father as best as he could. He is questioning a lot about his life as his father passed away less than two years ago, at the age of sixty-three. Reflecting on the fact that he is now half that age, he feels the sea has stolen years from his father, and his grandfather, not providing any chance for a peaceful end to their days. What is in store for him?

He is not the tallest of men, measuring just five foot seven, and as he sits quietly at the table, he cannot see over the kitchen windowsill to the children playing beyond. Hearing the joyful sounds of the children through the open windows, he rises from his chair to see into the garden and the scene succeeds in lifting him from his gloominess and indecision. Appreciating the living space around him, he knows it is a real pleasure to be here and he acknowledges the hard work that brought them to their new home. Adjusting to the size of the early Victorian building is a delight following the constraints of their previous home, and Robert enjoys wandering from room to room, taking in the freedom, imagining the children growing to fill their home. His decorating plans to improve the house are forming but he knows these will take time as he spends so many days at sea. Practical skills and hard work will not limit him as he looks forward to the challenge and effort needed.

The garden makes the biggest difference to their lives during the summer months, allowing the children the freedom to play and not be under their parents' feet. They have been blessed with three children, a daughter seven and two sons aged five and three. Watching them, he recollects how his brothers and sisters played together and the scrapes they got into.

His mood continues to lift as he thinks through his situation, and he knows that despite working hard in all weathers as a trawler skipper, he is doing the only job he has ever wanted to do. He has put pressure on his family by spending so much time away at sea, but it is a good living and recently the respectable income has allowed them to improve their situation.

Since the start of the war, Robert has focused on his reserved occupation and he has not been worried for a moment about being called up to serve. He is tough in body and spirit and like many experienced trawlermen he is playing a key role in feeding the country, earning a living in a harsh and dangerous environment. The physical demands of his job do not obviously match his thin and wiry frame, and many would not appreciate the steeliness that underpins his makeup. He has seen many lives claimed by the sea during his time on trawlers, and he has learnt to remember them fondly and use their memories to deal with the perils and maintain respect. Robert has lost many friends over the years and looking into his eyes you can see the depth of resilience that runs within him. He is not worried about being called up.

The kitchen table maintains its hold, as Robert sits and recalls his journey to become a deep-sea fisherman. His earliest recollections come from a time when he first sailed on trawlers out of his hometown. He was born in Fraserburgh, with its dominant position on the Scottish coast, jutting out into the harsh North Sea on the northeast corner of Aberdeenshire. His family benefitted from the Herring fishing industry that dominated the local economy during the early part of the twentieth century. The expansion of the harbour produced jobs that were filled by the inhabitants of this area and the town thrived.

Strong connections to the sea were formed early in his life as his family lived in Castle Street, sat next to the harbour, in close proximity to the fishing fleets, allowing him hours of play amongst the trawlers. Living in one of the small fishermen's cottages was a daily trial due to the cramped conditions and this drove Robert to do more for the family income. Indeed, he was keen to make his own way and it was a natural choice for him to become a fourth-generation trawlerman, taking great pride in the fishing traditions inherited from his father, grandfather and beyond. Everyone he knew or met in Fraserburgh was either a fisherman or someone connected to the fishing trade, so he fell in line.

In 1923, reaching the age of fourteen, he was already very familiar with the layout and operation of trawlers. Watching as they returned from trips at sea, he would ask to work on the decks while they were in the harbour. Helping the men, they taught him how to prepare nets, secure mooring lines and how to repair various parts of the ship. He helped gladly and appreciated watching the older fishermen go about their work, listening out for the stories they told of past trips out towards Iceland where the colossal seas claimed ships and men.

Memories of the occasion when his father took him out to fish for the first time are fixed firmly in his mind, as the mountainous sea created such a fearful experience. His immediate attention was on survival, but he also managed to observe the men on board, and he could not understand how they achieved any work in the conditions. As the ship pitched and rolled, he spent most of his energy trying to stay on his feet, while the experienced men used their innate ability to anticipate the motion and flex to continue their work with the nets at the stern, landing huge catches of Herring into the trawler's holds.

Winter trips to sea left their mark on him as salt, wind and ice toughened his skin and gave him lasting protection against the elements. Handling wet ropes in freezing conditions was painful and when numbness set in there were inevitable mistakes. Work cannot be delayed until the conditions improve, so to avoid injury or worse, the crew relied on each other to bring in the catch and stay safe. Lack of sleep and irregular meals added stress to the situation and eventually a week at sea left the men drained and exhausted.

Very keen eyesight helped Robert at sea, and he was often the first onboard to spy the Fraserburgh Lighthouse, signalling the way home from over twenty-two nautical miles away. In all his days at sea, he would never better that welcoming sight.

Links to the sea became ingrained in Robert even when he was not away fishing, as he would venture south of the town to the beautiful stretches of sandy beaches along the coast. There he enjoyed the solitude and the time away from the harsh demands of the fleet. He would walk amongst the sand dunes and use their height to stare far out to sea on a clear day. There he would sit and wonder where the sea would take him. What adventures would it have in store for a young lad who had not travelled far?

Learning the history and traditions of the area was important to him, and he discovered that before 1920 Herring fishing reached its peak and provided local families with a fair living. With the Great War behind them, the industry started to decline as there were fewer fishing crews available to operate the trawlers and everyone lamented the brave men who had not returned from serving in the Royal Navy or the Reserve. Robert had hoped to learn much of the war from the men who did return, but they never spoke of their experiences. As a young and inexperienced man, he did not understand the reticence of these heroes to relive their wartime years.

Over time Arctic and North Sea trips made a man of Robert, giving him the knowledge and experience necessary to be considered a trawlerman by the other men. As his experience and knowledge grew, so did the struggles of the fishing industry and in 1929 the lack of work forced him to move away from Fraserburgh to join a ship based at the major fishing port of Milford in West Wales. At the time the distance from his family mattered greatly to him. Later, his sister moved from Scotland to live nearby and that helped provide him with a sense of family. He was grateful for the chance to visit her and the opportunity to talk about the years they had spent growing up together.

His relocation caused many risks and challenges, but he faced them firmly and directly, learning the new ports, mastering challenging tides, and respecting new currents. New fishing grounds tested his confidence as often the catches were small or non-existent, but over time he built up his experience and the catch sizes followed. Being busy dissolved his doubts around the new life, but while everything was new, the long nights at sea provided plenty of time to play through his options and to reconsider his choices. Putting this early stage behind him, he began to feel at home on the new waters and as his confidence grew, he often experienced a calmness come over him when he saw the sea merge with a big sky on a clear day. Those clear days were rare, and he soon learnt how quickly the weather turned in that part of the world, rapidly changing the sea into a menacing and unpredictable state. Building his respect for the sea took years and was still needed every single day to keep him alive to the dangers. The sea provided a good living to those who grew up around it, and once it became a significant part of his life, it was hard to leave behind.

In Milford, Robert is known as the skipper of a new trawler called Fulmar. His crew watch him lead the vessel with reliability and sureness, as he stands in the wheelhouse, achieving his command with very few words. At sea he is confident and displays an inner strength that is not obvious to those that have not sailed with him.

Robert relishing his role as skipper as his wife builds a home in this beautiful part of Wales. He would not change this situation for anything in the world and he has no plans to uproot them and move back to Scotland.

Still finding comfort at the breakfast table he is stirred from his thoughts of the past when his wife enters the kitchen. Alice is a petite lady who breezes into the room knowing exactly where she would find her husband as he enjoys his tea, his newspaper, and a slow smoke. Dressed in her older working clothes she has her dark wavy hair tied up in a headscarf that shows signs of the paint she is applying to the front room. The tall ceilings of the rooms make the decorating a serious undertaking, but Alice has organised ladders and planking from her Father's business and has chosen not to take up his offers of help as she is determined to leave her mark on the decorating. Working hard, she balances the care of the children with her wish to see their house transformed into a fresh and bright home. Immersing herself in her work also helps as she tries to forget the path the war is taking, as she too is drawn to uncertain thoughts about the impact the conflict could have on their family.

Amused by her decorating clothes, Robert tries to raise a smile by comparing her look to some of the new fashions he has seen and doubts she will get away with that look in Chapel. Robert sees a determined look in her dark and deep-set eyes, realising he is already part of her plans for the day.

'What are you going to do today, Robert? I know it's Saturday, and you deserve your rest, but there are things to repair.'

'Yes, I know dear. I'm a bit sluggish today but I will do what I can.'

'Thank you.'

'I know I'm away at sea a lot and I haven't had much time to work on the house.'

'You do a hard job. I don't like asking you to do these repairs.'

'I want to make this house a good home for you all. What needs work?'

'If you could start with fitting the new hinges so the front room door will close properly.'

'Yes, that's where I'll start,' he adds, with little enthusiasm.

Driven and organised at sea, Robert is keen to move with a similar purpose on the house. He knows that Alice is also there to come to the fore and provide as much drive as himself. She wants a good home for the family and is not afraid of hard work.

Thinking about his wife, Robert is transported back to the time they met in early 1930. While running vessels out of the port of Milford, he was involved in local deliveries as well as going to sea for days on end. Often, he needed to distribute fish and other supplies to locations on Milford Haven, taking him to many of the small towns and communities along the waterway.

One of his favourite trips involved taking a small steam-powered trawler upstream from the port of Milford to the town of Pembroke. Delightfully different to the vast stretches of the open sea he would normally trawl, the Pembroke River trip required an intricate piece of navigation, as it presented a narrow and shallow channel to the helmsman. Familiarity counts and he used the landmarks of Bentlass and Jacob's Pill to help thread his steam-powered craft through the eye of the channel. Approaching Pembroke from the west, he enjoyed the historic scene of the Norman castle guarding the river in the final stages of the short six-mile journey.

Mooring up at Pembroke's south quay he organised the offloading of his cargo and distributed it amongst the waiting merchants. After his hard work, a good lunch could always be found at the George Hotel, right on the quayside. Knowing the hotel keeper well he always held back supplies of recently landed fish to offer the kitchens and increase his chances of good service. Over lunch, he often listened to a mixture of personal accounts and stories from across the county, as men from many backgrounds shared their tales over a pint of beer. Listening to the yarns, his lunchtimes go quickly, and he welcomes the comradery that has grown up over his many trips to the George.

Robert's frequent visits also mean he has noticed the lass who often serves him his lunch. Over the next few months, many conversations develop into courting and there is a rise in the frequency of his journeys to Pembroke. Alice is a slight and quiet girl, and she seems somewhat out of place working there, with all the bustle and leery behaviour you see in a town-based hostelry. Rushing about the hotel bar, Alice keeps on top of her work and occasionally steals a chance to speak to Robert. On one occasion they have a chance to sit and talk and discover how each other grew up and he learns that her father is a successful local plasterer. To his surprise, he learns that Alice's grandmother owned the hotel twenty years ago and that Alice had lived there for several years. She remained working there under the new owner but is looking to change the direction of her life.

Alice is nearly five years older than Robert and that takes him by surprise as that was not obvious to his close observation. Robert sees deeper than the quiet exterior and is struck by the feelings he has for Alice. Contrasting her nature to his, he is concerned that she will never fall for a tough and driven trawlerman, but he can tell she is very hardworking, and he wonders if that is where a great partnership can grow. Alice has less time to wait than Robert.

Many visits to the George allow them to get to know each other and soon they are set on a course to be together. Robert takes Alice out of the hotel and shows her more of his world with trips up the river and the chance to explain his job and his love of the sea. Treasuring these shared times together, Robert proposes and following a short engagement, they are married in 1932.

In the beginning, they share their lives together in a small cottage in Pembroke. Soon they face a growing problem, as all their space is gone, with three children arriving before the end of 1936. By

1939, Robert is offered the chance to Skipper his own trawler and this improvement allows them to afford a bigger house in Pembroke Dock. They welcome this lifeline, as it allows them to work on their family home and gives them the opportunity to create the best possible place for their children to grow up.

Settling into their new house is a delight, but the repair jobs have been mounting for months, with trips to sea consuming his time. Robert stirs from his seat, choosing to play with the children later. Prioritising the work he needs to do, he calls to Alice, 'Are those new door hinges in the front room?'

He meets Alice walking down the hallway with the new hinges in her hand.

'Here they are!' she says trying to remain light-hearted about expecting him to work on his day off.

Robert stops and turns. He stands in front of Alice and places his weathered hands on each of her shoulders. Alice is a head shorter than Robert and she looks upwards to meet his eyes as he pauses and stares back towards her. He asks Alice to come into the kitchen and sit down. Alerted to his seriousness, she is not sure what is on his mind as he pulls a folded letter from his trouser pocket. They both sit at the breakfast table and Robert starts to explain, 'this letter came in the post on Friday. I haven't found the right time to talk to you about it.'

Alice looks at him, with many thoughts racing through her mind. 'Please tell me what this is all about,' she asks with an intense look.

'It is a letter from the Royal Navy,' he adds without further elaboration.

'The Royal Navy,' repeats Alice.

'Yes, because I'm a registered Skipper and trawlerman, I've been asked to join the Royal Naval Patrol Service.'

'What's that, I've never heard of it.'

'Well, it's a new service created when the war started, and it allows trawlermen to join the navy and train quickly.'

'But I thought you'd carry on fishing for the war.'

'Well, the navy has taken over a lot of converted trawlers since the start of the war, and they need more crews. They want me to serve in one and help protect the coast.'

Alice has been avoiding any discussions of a call up because she knew his reserved occupation should count and keep him home. 'So, what does this involve?' she asks. 'Can you still be a local Skipper and do this?'

'No,' Robert hesitates. 'I need to give up my work here and leave to protect the English Channel and the North Sea.'

'But why go there to do that! Doesn't this coast here need to be protected?'

'I can't answer that. The Royal Navy need experienced seamen to protect the Channel because that is where the work is, especially with all the talk of invasion.'

Taking his time, Robert explains that the Royal Navy formed this service and are looking for experienced seamen to join the new naval recruits that are currently going through basic training. He feels good about being selected and recognises how well he can cope with the new job he is expected to do. Alice worries immediately about the distance between the two of them and how the children will miss their father. Robert admits to feeling similar emotions, as their conversation continues for most of the morning. Thinking back to the time when he first moved to Wales and how he missed his Scottish family, he now worries that his new family will not cope with the change he is forcing on them.

A moment of clarity comes to him while he sits at the breakfast table, his mind is made up, and he must serve his country in the best way he can.

Alice's head is full of upheaval and she focuses on very practical matters. Her real concerns are for her husband and the challenges he will face, both physical and emotional. Having been brought up in a rural location, her early years have taught her to be practical and reliable. Robert has many of the same traits and his steadfastness and dependability are what drew her to him in the beginning. Recently, since the children have been born, Robert has had problems keeping things in perspective. Potential problems concerning the children have been amplified beyond any normal and reasonable consideration and eventually this has led to an over cautious response to daily events. Staying on top of these emotions is very hard for Robert and leaving home is only going to make matters worse and amplify his anxiety. Alice finds solace by knowing that he will immerse himself in his work and control his emotions that way. On recent trips to sea, the immediate separation is an emotional wrench, but his confidence soon returns when he is back at home, with new stories to recount and previous perilous tales to update to new versions.

Currently, many women are in very similar circumstances to Alice, but they are more likely to be concerned with various matrimonial or more intimate considerations. For Alice, her struggle is managing her husband's safe transition from a family man to a seafarer at war.

Chapter 2

Family Time

2nd August 1940, Milford Haven

The trawler Fulmar cuts through the swell as St Anne's Head lighthouse passes on the starboard side. The crew are readying the ship for a short trip to sea so Robert can show the new Skipper how the trawler handles and how well the crew work together. Feeling this is his trawler, Robert knows the crew are shaped by his thinking and they operate the ship to his system. He is not happy, but he cannot complain as he has brought about the need for the change of skipper.

The Fulmar's owner met with Robert two days earlier and the conversation did not linger on the decision he had made to join up. Finding a new skipper became the priority and both men agreed that no one in the current crew had the experience to take over. This meant a new skipper had to be found from the men based out of other Milford Haven trawlers. New skipper positions attract a lot of interest because the leader of the ship takes home a higher percentage of the profits based on the landed catch size and sale price. The lion's share is taken by the owner but that is not begrudged by anyone as he shoulders the burden of all the costs.

The owner's choice for a new skipper is an experienced hand from the other ship he owns so the decision to keep it in the firm makes sense and Robert agreed to organise a sea trip to help everyone with the transition.

Standing in the Fulmer's wheelhouse, Robert watches the crew as they carry out their duties while he keeps a quiet eye on Dobson, the new skipper. Dobson has more years at sea than Robert and is a few years older than him, but that counts for nothing as far as he is concerned.

Robert has mapped out the day from their departure at 0600 to their return that evening. His favourite fishing grounds are off the southwest coast of Ireland but that involves a trip lasting a few days. His simpler plan is to steam for four hours, trawl for another four and then head for home. Handing the ship over to Dobson he stands back in the wheelhouse and watches the outing unfold.

It is a bright and sunny summers day and Robert has a relaxing morning, enjoying the journey to the area selected on the charts. Dobson has the trawler completely and safely under his control and the atmosphere aboard is calm and pleasant, reflecting the sea conditions they are enjoying. The first trawl of the day nets a small catch of Haddock and Plaice and this is judged as a good result for such shallow waters. Dobson is showing remarkably good command of the vessel and Robert feels some weight lift from his shoulders as he realises that he can leave the trawler in his capable hands and the world will keep on turning.

The peaceful journey back to Milford is soon interrupted by a magnificent sight and sound. Approaching from the east they spot a Short Sunderland and watch in fascination as the mighty flying boat starts to fill their view, taking a path directly towards their position. The crew follow the aircraft as it travels at a low altitude, enabling it to spot U-Boats waiting in the Western Approaches for Allied shipping convoys. Passing low and to the port side of the trawler, the Sunderland's four Pegasus engines put out a raw sound that leaves those on the Fulmar shocked and awestruck. Enthralled by the sight, Robert's thoughts are with the airmen aboard the flying boat as they are engaged doing what he wants to do now more than anything. Defend the country.

Robert collects his paper early on Friday morning and starts his return to the house. The short walk takes him up Charlton Place and turning into Victoria Road he looks over to the two large dockyard hangars and immediately feels another connection to the role he has signed up for on the other side of the country. The two hangars are used by RAF Coastal Command to maintain the squadrons of Short Sunderlands, one of which passed over them at sea a few days ago. His mind wanders as he considers the skills he has and how useful they could be working on the haven, running tugs and tenders to manage the growing fleet of flying boats. He could do an excellent job working with the Sunderlands, and he could stay at home, but he jolts himself back to the reality of his choice and looks towards his role with the RNPS. Using his skills and experience to mould new recruits and turn them into the crew of a new ship is a much better service to the country. He stops fighting in his own mind and rests on the convictions of his choice for this war.

Settling at the kitchen table, with the rest of the household upstairs, Robert's morning cup of tea and his newspaper take all his attention as the day continues in a comfortable fashion. Hearing the familiar sound of the letterbox open and close, he moves quickly to see what has been delivered. Days of waiting for a letter from the navy have been rewarded as he opens the brown envelop and sees the joining instructions he has been expecting.

Sat back at the kitchen table he pauses before taking in the details enclosed. The date is set, and he is to report to the RNPS station in Lowestoft in just eight days' time, on Sunday 18th August. Various documents are enclosed but holding the travel permit in his hand is the one that catapults him forward to the point where he must leave and separate himself from his family.

Looking up to see Alice standing in the doorway, their eyes connect and each of them is easily able to tell the other's thoughts. Alice joins him at the table, and he fills in the details from the letter. Robert must leave on the first train on Saturday morning, so they seize the chance to plan the time they have together, giving them eight days to enjoy the most of their time together with the children. James, their youngest, has his fourth birthday on the 19th August and that cruel piece of timing hits them both hard. In her usual manner, Alice is quick to soften the blow and announces a special party for Friday as an early celebration.

Passing quickly, the weekend involves very little out of their normal routine. Not spending weeklong trips at sea shows how difficult it is for Robert to relax as he carries on with maintenance jobs around the house.

Tuesday dawns and Robert rises refreshed from one of the best night's sleep he has had in quite a while. They decide to take a bus into Pembroke knowing the children will love the twenty-minute journey with their little faces pressed up against the windows, watching the world go by. Their excitement grows when they see the castle in the distance as the bus descends the hill and approaches the town. There is a chorus of, 'are we going in Daddy?' and Robert tells them they must pay a visit to have some lunch first and then they will go into the castle. His announcement does not sink in for a while, but then they realise and excitedly ask, 'are we seeing Granny and Grandad?'

'Yes', replies Alice. The children are delighted to hear that, but they are still fixated on the Norman castle that dominates the west of the town. Getting off the bus at The Green, they walk towards the Mill

Bridge. Within a minute more excitement surfaces as they approach the George Hotel. The children know this is where they see their grandparents and where they get to play with their cousins. Alice has been arranging this from the moment she knew Robert was leaving. Although they are visiting her family, she knows he feels very comfortable here and he gets on well with her sister and her family. A big lunch has been arranged and a great welcome awaits Robert as the details of his sign up have been provided by Alice to the rest of the family.

Alice joins her sister, and their children play together, while Alice's father, Henry, gets Robert a drink and invites him to sit at a table close to a window. Henry has done well for himself by building up a small plastering business and he was in much demand before war was declared. Robert is unsure how close Henry is to retiring but he knows he has done well for himself and always looks flush. Apart from his external looks, it is easy to see where Alice gets her small frame and height from. Henry turns toward Robert.

'How are you son?'

'Very good, thank you. I'm glad to have a chance to see you all today.'

'Yes, it's great to be able to get together. How long will it take you to get to your port?'

'It's a long journey and can take fourteen hours on different trains. The length of the journey struck me when I first held the travel permit.'

'I was going to ask you when you plan to leave, but that's a bad Pembrokeshire habit we have. It's the first thing we ask someone as soon as we've met them.'

'I'm used to that now. I'm due at the base Sunday evening so I have to catch the first train out Saturday morning, and stopover in London the first night.'

'What can you tell me about what you'll be doing?'

'I'm not sure what I can tell you that you won't have already seen in the papers. I'm joining a converted Trawler to patrol the Channel and the North Sea for enemy craft or possibly join a minesweeper.'

'Well, it's good to know you will be out there protecting us.'

'Thank you,' responds Robert and he feels himself lifted by the very simple acknowledgement of his upcoming work.

The two men are called to the table for lunch and the family all join in the feast that has been laid on.

Hugs and kisses have more significance than usual, as they come to say goodbye following a hearty lunch. Robert feels he is embraced for longer and harder than normal.

They walk slowly up the hill to the castle entrance. Once inside the children run around and use up energy that Robert does not possess following his lunch and a couple of welcome pints of beer.

There are many turrets and battlements to explore, and Robert and Alice must keep up as best they can as the walls have sheer drops on one side or the other. Everyone has broad smiles on their faces as they make their way back to the bus stop. As soon as they are on the bus the children fall asleep on their parents' laps and Robert and Alice talk of the new memories they can share while apart.

Robert has planned a surprise for Wednesday as he arranged to borrow Henry's car when they met the previous day. Telling Alice he has to go and see someone, he slips out of the house straight after breakfast. A short bus journey transports him to The Green in Pembroke and partway along his short walk to the hotel, he spots the car parked up outside the George. He meets Henry and is given the keys to an Austin 7 Ruby saloon. The car is Henry's pride and joy, and Robert is reluctant to take the responsibility of driving it, but Henry had offered and insisted that he have the car for a family day out. Feeling this is some type of reward based on their conversation over lunch, he gratefully accepts.

Returning to his house he calls the family to the front door and pointing to the car he announces they are going on a family day out. He asks Alice to prepare a small picnic and it is not long before they fill the car and are heading off. There are many beautiful beaches within a fifteen-minute drive of Pembroke Dock, and some are so secluded they need a cliff walk and steep climb to reach. Their choice today is Freshwater East as it is close and a safe beach for all the family to enjoy. Unaware of their destination, the children are very excited and more than happy to simply watch the world go by from the rear of this magical machine.

After a short walk from the parked car, they reach the golden sand and see the tide out, creating a vast area to run around. The water's edge is the main draw for the children, and they show their excitement by almost dragging their parents towards the sea. It is a bright summer day and shoes and socks are abandoned for a paddle in the water. Running in and out of the tide, the children create joyous screams as they feel the cold of the water on their legs. With the tide turning there are small waves for them to jump over. Following that excitement, they make their way over to the righthand side of the beach where there are rock pools left by the receding tide. It is such a joy for Robert and Alice to help the children explore the pools that teem with sea life. Exploring many pools before the tide comes in, the children are fascinated as they uncover crabs, tiny fish, and the occasional shrimp.

Soon everyone is hungry, and the picnic does its best to fill their outdoor appetites. Sand dunes are the next places to explore, and Robert tries to shepherd the three young adventurers as they climb and swoop amongst the tall grass. It is a large game of hide-n-seek and Alice watches from the beach as her heart is filled with the joy of their togetherness.

A day full of carefree happiness, and the car trip home, leaves the children asleep. Alice is delighted with the surprise for the day and she thanks Robert for the effort he has gone to. He simply thanks her for the great family time they have had together.

That evening Robert arranges to see two of his friends who also work on trawlers. They meet in a local pub and find they have so much to discuss. Robert learns the names of the men that have already volunteered from the local area, and also of the men who are under forty-two who have been conscripted to the different services. His two drinking companions tell him that they are all working hard to bring fish into the harbour, but they are missing some very experienced skippers like himself. There are a lot of fishing crews learning the hard way and getting their experience from those who do not have many years at sea themselves. Robert takes time to explain his motivations for signing up, and how the RNPS works but stops short of trying to persuade either of them to volunteer. Each man has his own reasons for the way they want to serve, and he would not want to persuade anyone to go to war, and then be killed or wounded when they are already serving the country in a dangerous occupation. Robert does not stay too long with his friends as he knows his time at home is precious.

Thursday follows a slow relaxing pattern as it starts with a fulsome breakfast. Their time together allows for lots of fun with the children and some quiet time for them both. Robert takes the children for a walk to the end of the Fort Road where there is a pebble beach and there is a great chance to throw stones into the haven. Robert is pleasantly surprised to be standing by this imposing stretch of water so close to his home. He talks to the children as they try to throw stones the furthest distance and they are soon jumping with joy as he shows them how to make a flat stone skim across the water. They try to copy this with little success and call repeatedly for him to repeat the magic.

Friday arrives and there is a party to organise for James. Simple party food is made, and the birthday boy plays with little knowledge of the fuss being made. The older children enjoy helping with the food and Robert hides the emotional pressure he is feeling.

As the day passes there are little items that start to tug at his emotions. Washing is folded and placed near his kit bag and he is asked if he wants to take a packed lunch with him for the journey. The children are put to bed and he and Alice share a quiet time together, talking about the future, the risks, the dangers and even venture into the area of what they should do should something tragic happen.

'It has been so good to have you home in the past few days, Robert. The children have adored seeing you.'

'Yes, they are growing up so fast. It is hard being away while you must look after them. I'm struggling with the distance and not being here in case anything happens.'

'But what could happen?'

'Well, the war has made me think of all sorts of things that can go wrong. There will be many long nights on patrol and there are times when I know I will feel helpless.'

'Don't feel helpless. I'm sure you will be very busy, but you will soon be back on leave to visit us. We are safe here and I do get help from my sister.'

'I know. I'm fine with any danger at sea, but the children always make me think of things very differently.'

'Well, know that I'm here looking after them and you are looking after us and so much more. Now let's call it a night. You have a very early start in the morning.'

'Yes, let's go to bed.'

Chapter 3

Setting Off to War

17th August 1940, West Wales

Hobb's Point is a large concrete slipway sitting on the edge of the haven. The family are gathered there to see Robert begin his journey to the other side of the country. This is not the most obvious place to start his journey, as trains leave directly from Pembroke Dock station, but during wartime everyone has stopped expecting things to be done in the most straightforward way. Robert's train leaves from the GWR station in Neyland, but first he must take the passenger ferry, Lady Magdalene, across the waterway. This journey is very familiar to Robert, but today it has a dramatically different significance, and he is glad fewer passengers are travelling than usual.

Tensions exist between Robert and Alice, but they have both agreed to make their goodbyes as easy as they can for each other. Knowing this is hard for Robert, Alice moves to keep the goodbyes as modest and muted as she can, hoping to minimise his distress and reduce his thoughts of separation. Conflicted, Alice is focusing on his needs while attempting to suppress her own turmoil. Knowing he could stay home and help the war effort, her feelings do not sit well with her, and the great unspoken truth is that Robert has matching feelings. Adding to his own confusion, he talks of the impending separation in the same way he normally describes a week-long fishing trip to sea. She recognises the strain.

Noticing the ferry is preparing to leave, Alice deflects the conversation and moves the children towards their father. They are too young to detect their parents' emotions and they continue to enjoy the adventures of a trip to see the ferry. Saying their goodbyes, Alice and the children are lovingly embraced, as Robert finally boards the small ship.

Standing next to the rail at the stern, Robert watches the release of the temporary mooring lines and looks to the funnel as the steam engine first drives forward from the side of the slipway and then quickly turns towards the opposite bank of the haven. He is facing back towards the slipway and waves to his lovely family as they stand behind the railings. His heart is heavy as the slow motion of the ferry prolongs the agony of the situation. Everyone waves frantically as they disappear into the distance. Hanging on to the sight of his family, he waits until they turn and start their walk home before he faces the opposite shore.

Robert is full of purpose as he boards his train. Moving towards his compartment, he is suddenly aware of the other passengers in the corridor and those sitting around the seat he has picked out. Wondering why the train is so busy he stows his luggage, takes his seat, and settles in for the long journey to London. It is four weeks since he told Alice that he had signed up.

Looking at his travel warrant he wonders what is ahead of him. The arrangements cover both stages of his journey to the capital and beyond, with the inclusion of bed and breakfast near Paddington for a stopover that evening.

He has never been to London before and arriving after a long journey he is struck by the size of the terminus. It is late evening and there are still many people transiting through the station as he stops and stands to one side to search for the copy of a map he was sent. The map directs him to a townhouse just half a mile from the station. Walking down the street, he trails another man who seems to be following a similar map. Stopping at the same door, they exchange a simple greeting and show each other their copy of the same typed instructions.

The front door opens, and the landlady welcomes them both into the hall of a plain and functional looking house that has many signs of high traffic. She delivers a very well-rehearsed speech that sets out the house rules before they are shown to their individual rooms on the second floor. Robert settles into his room, deciding not to unpack as he is moving on to Lowestoft in the morning. Hunger takes a firm grip, as he realises his only food that day was a sandwich bought during a short stop at Bristol.

There is a knock at his door and opening it he faces the man he had just met at the front door.

'Hello, pleased to meet you, my name is James … James Fredricks'

'Hello James, pleased to meet you. My name is Robert Crawford.'

'I know it's late, but I am heading out to get a drink and a sandwich. Would you like to join me?'

Robert hesitates and then said, 'Are you joining up?'

Well, I'm already in the Royal Navy and I'm heading off to Lowestoft in the morning. How about you?'

'I work on trawlers, and I'm heading to Lowestoft tomorrow, to join the Patrol Service.'

'I'd heard that they were bringing navy trained people together with experienced seamen. I'm trained as a gunner and volunteered to be transferred to the RNPS. Let's go for that drink.'

Based on their shared destination Robert agrees, and they head out to a pub on the corner of the road they had walked along earlier. It is a good chance for both men to swap the stories of how they joined up and the basic pub sandwiches are very welcome.

'How did you end up in the navy,' asks Robert.

'Well, I come from a naval family and my father served in the last war, so I've grown up with all his stories and decided to join up. That was before war broke out but here I am fully trained, and I've got a head start.'

'What did you train for,' asks Robert.

'I did my basic training, and then I signed up for my gunnery training.'

Robert is conscious that he is asking all the questions, but he has one more he wants to ask, 'so why transfer from the full navy to the RNPS?'

Taking a drink, James pauses, 'well, we heard they were setting up the RNPS and that there was a real need to protect the coast and the channel. They talked about U-Boats and mines being a problem today, so a few of us decided we'd like to see action now and not wait for months for anything to happen. But what about you. Why did you join up?'

Robert answers as best as he can. 'It was a sense of duty to me. I'm an experienced trawlerman and I was thinking I could serve out the war bringing in fish. But then I realised there was a bigger job to do. I want to protect this country from the evil I see. It's about good and evil for me.'

'I can understand that,' says James, rising to get another beer. 'Same again?'

'Yes, go on, but can I have a whisky?' replies Robert as if he is having his arm twisted. 'But this is the last one as I'll need to be wide awake for tomorrow's journey.'

James puts the new drinks down, retakes his seat and asks, 'So where do you come from?'

'Originally, I'm from Scotland. But now I live in a town called Pembroke Dock, in West Wales.'

'That's a long way to travel. Have you always been a trawlerman?'

'Yes,' replies Robert, telling James about his early years fishing off Scotland and his move to fish off Wales.

'So, you've sailed in some big seas then?'

'Oh yes, I've got some stories to tell.'

'You're looking for something calmer in the Channel or the North Sea then?'

'Well let's see what the winter has in store. I don't know the southern part of the North Sea or the Channel so I'm guessing it's calmer than being off Iceland, but I'm not sure.'

'I see, well let's hear some of those stories?' asks James.

Robert obliges with a number of his best stories of making a hard living out at sea. James is impressed, but it does not take them long and soon it is time to return to their digs.

Early morning arrives and both men eat their breakfast quietly as the landlady attends to other paying guests. Having gathered his things together first thing, Robert is ready, but he asks James if he wants to travel to Liverpool Street Station with him and they agree to meet outside in fifteen minutes. Robert finishes his tea and James returns to his room.

The landlady provides details of the right bus to get them to Liverpool Street station on the other side of London. Travelling on the bus through the early morning traffic, Robert takes in all the sights around him and concludes that the capital is prepared for war. Most of the signs are visible, but there are also a few subtle and less obvious signs, visible to anyone with a keen eye. Robert notices the details in things, always seeing beyond the obvious. He notices two soldiers standing sentry duty outside a building that would not normally demand a second look. The country is changing as the war takes its grip and his thoughts turn to how safe his family is going to be. He begins to feel better when he considers their distance from the capital and the relative unimportance of where they live.

Their transit through Liverpool Street goes smoothly. Sitting on the Lowestoft train they speak occasionally about what they expect to encounter when they arrive. Robert looks around the carriage and weighs up the other men seated there, assuming the majority are heading for the RNPS base. Arriving at Lowestoft station they find navy trucks ready to take them directly to the base listed on their travel documents and after a short journey of just over a mile, they arrive at the RNPS depot, located at a place called Sparrow's Nest.

Arriving at the depot, Robert is surprised alongside the other recruits, as they discover the layout of the site next to the sea. In contrast, they know this is the country's most easterly location, and they feel very close to the war.

The base is known as the Sparrow's Nest, and the priority is to register with the main office and collect his uniform and kit from the stores. Some men are living in the Nest's converted concert hall but others like Robert are given the name and address of a bed and breakfast billet. Following a general talk from a senior officer, the men are dismissed for the rest of the day.

Talking to the assembled men, the senior officer lets them know that they will receive details of their training schedule directly after Colours the following morning. For the first of many occasions, Robert is left thinking he has a lot to learn about navy ways. He decides to get something to eat at the NAAFI before finding transport to his billet. Finding someone to ask about Colours is his next challenge, and fortunately there are a few new recruits milling around a Petty Officer explaining that Colours is the ceremony that starts each day in the navy, whether you are at sea or ashore. At this time of year, Colours is at eight o'clock in the morning and from this conversation the new recruits get their first lesson in naval tradition. As they continue to eat and drink, there are opportunities for the men to say hello and to exchange stories of where they have travelled from. The conversations do not go on for long as the men are asked to catch one of the navy trucks that are starting to leave the Nest to drop them at their billets.

Robert finds his digs are very basic and similar to the bed and breakfast he stayed at in London. He does not know it yet, but he is very fortunate and has a good allocation of accommodation. Many of the men arriving at the Nest are being put in digs that do not meet the most basic of standards. There is little time to complain, and some landladies exploit the situation, happily taking money from the next collection of men passing through the town. Robert's landlady is chatty and kind but most of all determined to have the coupons from his ration book. The navy is paying for accommodation and food, but without the ration book coupons, there is little hope of a good hearty breakfast or an additional evening meal.

The evening passes quickly as he tries on his uniform and checks through all the equipment he has been given. Eager to get started on his training, he attempts to second guess the drills they will be given to learn the following day. The earlier talk from the senior officer had explained how the navy trainees are being handled separately from the men like himself who have sea experience. In the short time available, navy trainees are to be taken off the coast on exercises to help them gain as much sea experience as possible. At the same time, the experienced trawlermen and seafarers are to be trained in the ways of the navy. This involves command structures, communication systems, weaponry, and all manner of ways to run a ship the navy way. New recruits from both sides of this training are due to come together in two weeks to be assigned to a crew and then allocated to a ship.

Chapter 4

The Fire

19th August 1940, Pembroke Dock

Low cloud covers the North Sea and there is a misty, dampening rain falling over a wide area. Although inconvenient, the rain does little harm, leaving the low cloud to play an acute role at this stage in the Battle of Britain. In these conditions, mass bombing formations cannot fly and there is a marked reduction in the number of Luftwaffe raids on RAF airstrips in the south of England. With this reduced visibility, the enemy shifts its plans by organising many small raids, each attacking strategic coastal targets.

Enemy light bombers fly on small sorties from airstrips in occupied France, and on the morning of 19th August 1940, one such flight departs to travel across the South West counties of England before turning towards targets in West Wales. During this raid, a Junkers JU88 bomber arrives at the head of Milford Haven and turns east to line up on its target. Travelling down the large natural harbour there is little in the way of defensive fire to distract it from its deadly aim.

Sitting either side of the town of Pembroke Dock, are two Admiralty Fuel Storage Depots, each one containing large quantities of fuel, ready to supply the navy. Following months of demand from Atlantic and coastal convoys, there are fuel shortages and the country's strategic depots each hold an increasingly precious wartime resource. One of the Pembroke Dock depots sits inland close to the top of the town and uses underground pipes to deliver fuel to jetties in the dockyard where naval and merchant ships can be refuelled.

The Junkers aircraft lines up on the inland depot at Llanreath and approaches on a low run to release its cargo of bombs. Only one bomb finds its target and explodes close to the base of one of the eighteen large fuel tanks. The explosion ignites thousands of tons of fuel oil in a partly filled tank and the race begins to protect the other tanks, many holding much larger volumes of fuel. No one is prepared for this level of danger and destruction.

Monday is rather dull, and looking skyward, Alice cannot decide if it is going to rain. It is the middle of the school holidays and the children are in the garden happily occupying themselves without complaint. The children know it is James' birthday and they join in the fun to spoil him, while Alice uses her time to write to Robert, hoping he settles into his new base, especially as this is his first day of training. Writing about the children and their happy play is a good start to the first page, but she soon runs out of ideas as they only said goodbye two days ago. The laughter from the garden is a strong pull so Alice leaves the house to spend time playing with the children.

Without warning, a thunderous noise fills the air as Alice simultaneously hears the noise and feels the accompanying shock wave. Without knowing the cause, she assumes there is an explosion close by and immediately ushers the children from the garden into the safety of the house. Following advice, they need to take shelter fast. Fortunately, their Victorian house has a decent sized cellar to use as an air-raid shelter, so Alice moves everyone towards the door underneath the staircase and carefully guides them down the warn and uneven concrete steps. The cellar is poorly lit, remaining cold despite the time of year and it is not the safest environment for the children as Robert has used it as a workshop while working on the house. Sensing the alarm from their mother's actions the children begin to cry and pull at her dress. Alice speaks softly to calm them and attempts to get them all to say nursery rhymes to take their mind off the air raid that is happening above.

There is something unexplained and unsettling about being in the cellar and waiting for the next detonation to shake their nerves. Alice cannot understand the lack of further explosions that you would expect from an ongoing air raid. The proximity of the house to the dockyard, and the location of squadrons of Sunderland flying boats, had caused her to worry in the past. The anti-submarine Sunderlands are an obvious target for a daytime raid but there have not been any in the past, so it is difficult to know what to expect. She is puzzled.

The cellar has an opening at pavement level that is protected by an iron grating. Beneath the grating is a void that slopes away from the cellar and a sash window that keeps the weather from entering the underground room. Finding the window stiff to open, Alice eventually manages to lower the top pane so she can hear any activity from the street. At first, there is silence but listening carefully she starts to hear the fire engines' bells as they make their way to the dockyard. Soon they will pass directly in front of the house as they take a direct route to the main dockyard gate. Time passes and the fire bells fade rather than grow leading her to the conclusion that this has nothing to do with the dockyard. Ideally, a view from the upstairs bedrooms would confirm any activity but she cannot leave the children alone in the cellar with all the tools, or if there should be another explosion.

As the minutes pass she wonders how she will know that it is safe to leave their current shelter. Staring through the pavement grating there is a sight that confuses her even more. A massive cloud of very dark smoke is rising into the sky from the direction of the Defensible Barracks.

This imposing building is a twenty-sided stone fort, complete with moat, built a hundred years ago to protect the town and its Royal Dockyard. Currently, the fort houses the military forces assigned to the protection of Milford Haven.

Dominating the skyline when viewed from the town, the fort is an impressive sight. With the huge clouds of dark smoke rising behind it, a more apt description would be terrifying.

Quickly, Alice realises that the fort is not the target of the bombs or the source of the smoke. The fort is directly in the line of sight between her house and the oil tanks that sit on the far side of what the locals call the Barrack Hill. This explains the fire engines not passing her door, as instead they must have headed towards the oil tanks via a road that lies on the opposite side of Barrack Hill. Realising the oil tanks are the target, Alice takes the children back to the kitchen and arranges for them to have some sandwiches as an early tea and to keep them occupied. A knock at the door takes Alice out of the kitchen but she moves carefully not to excite the little ones. She opens the door to her neighbour who is now standing on the pavement, pointing up the hill to the sight of the ever-growing clouds of thick, dark smoke. An ugly shadow is being cast on the town. The ladies talk for a while and are joined by others as they come out of their houses to stand and stare from their doorsteps, unsure what to make of the hellish sight. The oil tanks are half a mile away from the Crawford's house, but they cannot be seen directly as the hill forms a natural barrier. The closeness is alarming.

Alice is making herself busy, putting the children to bed, when there is a knock at the door. A policeman stands there, and as her heart leaps into her throat, she immediately thinks of Robert and how this must be bad news.

'What's happened Office?' asks Alice missing out on any pleasantries.

'Well, Madam. We're visiting house-to-house to explain what has happened to the oil tanks at the Llanreath depot. A bomber came up the haven and one of its bombs hit a tank. The explosion has set fire to thousands of tonnes of fuel oil and that's the smoke you can see.'

'Was anyone hurt?' is Alice's first question as she is still in some shock and thinking of Robert.

'No, fortunately no one was hurt. The local fire brigade is there trying to stop the fire from spreading to other tanks. I think there are eighteen other tanks in total.'

'So, it could get worse?'

'Well, we don't know yet Madam. We're telling everyone to close their windows in case the wind changes direction and the smoke starts heading for the town.'

'Right, I'll do that straight away. Are we going to be evacuated?'

'No plans for that Madam. Please stay put.'

'What about the houses in Pennar they must be so close to the fire. I have friends living there.'

'Yes, we're having to move some people from houses there but no other places at the moment. I must move on now Madam as there are others to speak to. Please wait for other instructions and stay inside.'

'Thank you, Officer. Good evening.'
'Good evening Madam.'

Alice passes through the house checking all the windows knowing that they were all shut earlier, due to the unusually dull and breezy August day. The children are in bed and have fortunately fallen asleep with little fuss. A glow in the southern sky can be seen from the upstairs windows and Alice cannot settle knowing the danger that lies over the hill. Thinking of Robert, she knows he is not aware of what is happening, but the news will travel to Lowestoft via the newspapers, and it will not be long before he finds out. The letter she started must be finished.

Waking early the following morning, Alice moves straight for her bedroom window to draw back the curtains to reveal the skyline. The smoke clouds are larger, darker, and more menacing than the night before. A crowd has gathered at the top of the hill, next to the Defensible Barracks and she is drawn to join them, but she is not going to scare or endanger the children by leaving the house, even under the watchful eye of a neighbour. Setting about the task of waking the children and giving them breakfast, she plans the day well so there are distractions and ways to avoid staring out of the windows. A neighbour kindly agrees to post her letter.

It is mid-afternoon and there is a knock at the door. A different policeman is standing there with two other men, both looking dirty and exhausted in their firemen's uniforms.

'Good afternoon Madam.'

'Good afternoon Officer.'

'We're asking people along this street to kindly take in firemen who are fighting the oil tank fires.'

'Haven't they got their own homes to go to?'

'These firemen are not from here Madam. The chief fire officer has called in brigades from all over Wales to tackle the fire. I think there are over a dozen brigades here already and there are more coming tomorrow. Where are you boys from?'

'We're from Swansea, Officer. Sorry to disturb you Madam we realise that people do not know how many brigades have been called in to fight this fire.'

'We just need a place to sleep and a place to wash up if you can help?' add the other fireman in a tired and weary voice.

'Yes, I can help. I have a spare room, which is not even decorated, but you're welcome to sleep there.'

'Thank you, Madam. I'll leave the firemen with you to sort out the arrangements as I need to find more help.'

'Come this way,' invites Alice and the men follow, first removing their filthy and heavy boots at the door.

'There is a room upstairs at the back of the house you can use. There isn't a bed, but I can find some blankets for you. It's also right next to the bathroom.'

'Thank you, Madam. We appreciate what you're doing for us and we'll try to keep out of your way.'

'That's fine. Please remember I have three young children in the house, so I'd appreciate as little noise as possible.'

'We'll be as quiet as we can be.'

Alice shows the men the room and the bathroom next door. She fetches some blankets and some towels and leaves them at the door as the men put some of their uniforms on the floor in the corner of the room.

'We're off for eight hours since two o'clock so we'll be leaving at ten o'clock tonight. We won't be back until two o'clock tomorrow afternoon.'

'I see. Will you want some food?'

'No thank you. We don't want to be any trouble.'

'I'll find you something. Do you want to eat before getting some sleep?'

'Yes, please. That is very kind. We'll have a wash and then join you.'

Alice returns to the kitchen and prepares some eggs, bacon, and bread for the firemen. She is worried that Robert would not be happy with the idea of strange men in the house, but she has agreed to them staying now and there is no point worrying about it.

The men arrive downstairs and find the food being laid on the table.

'Thank you,' says the older man. 'I'm Albert John by the way, and this fellow is Wynn Davies.'

'Hello, pleased to meet you. I'm Mrs Alice Crawford.'

'Thank you, Mrs Crawford. This is very kind of you.'

'Please sit down. Now, can you tell me what is happening with the fire?'

'Well, it's serious. There is a lot of fuel there and we are trying to stop the fire from spreading to different tanks. There are four tanks on fire already, so it's spread since the first tank was hit by the bomb. There are so many firemen there, it is quite a sight.'

'I see. My husband is away at the moment. He's with the Royal Naval Patrol Service.'

'That is a difficult job,' says Albert. 'My brother is a trawlerman out of Swansea docks and he's just joined up with the Patrol Service. He left for Lowestoft about a month ago.'

'That's a coincidence,' adds Alice, now feeling better about having the firemen in the house with their fishing connections. 'My husband has just started at Lowestoft. He only left last Saturday and I'm missing him terribly.'

'Was he a trawlerman before he signed up?'

'Yes, he skippered a local trawler and had been fishing in Scotland before that.'

'He's like my brother then. Sea in his veins.'

'Yes. They are good for the Patrol Service as they are used to spending days at sea and working very hard.'

'Yes, they do. You must be proud of him.'

'Yes, I am.'

The firemen retire for some sleep and Alice starts another letter to Robert. She realises that news of the current situation must have reached Lowestoft based on the newspaper coverage, so she is in no doubt that he has heard of the fire. She also knows that he will be worrying because of the short distances involved when comparing the position of their house to the location of the tanks. Covering most of the facts, her letter mentions the firefighting effort in some detail, but she also tempers the scale of the disaster, as too much reality would be sure to drive more concern. She hopes her second letter reaches the base as quickly as possible, and she is optimistic that she can help to calm his fears.

Her letter does not mention the firemen who have been billeted with her as Robert is quite old fashioned in his views of what is reasonable to expect of a woman living in a house without her husband. Alice takes the view that she oversees the house now that he is away, and it is for her to decide what is right and necessary to support the war effort.

Reading about the new roles for women in the WRNS or WAFF she understands the logic of freeing up men from the shore-based Royal Navy stations or the aircrew for the RAF. She is convinced that women can do more in this war than just look after their homes and raise their children. She has family close by who could look after the children if she could find the right role for herself. She is determined to do more before this war is over.

By Thursday morning the fire has raged for three nights and there is no sign of it being distinguished in the next few days. Supporting the effort to fight the fire is something Alice is proud to do, but she is glad the men leave the house at ten o'clock, as she can lock up and not worry about strangers in the house overnight. There is a lot of explaining to do to the children as their inquisitive minds want to know why there has been so much happening over the past few days. The boys are fascinated with the idea of firemen being in the house but they are told that the men are working hard and must not be disturbed while they sleep.

The men return each afternoon following sixteen straight hours fighting the conflagration. Welcoming any food that is offered, there is only a brief opportunity for Alice to pick up information about the fire before they take to their makeshift beds. Twenty-two brigades are now involved in fighting the blaze and over six hundred men have been drafted in, some coming from all over Wales, Bristol, and Birmingham to fight the biggest fire the country has seen. One afternoon, early in their stay the men return in an extremely sombre mood. After some awkward silence, they tell Alice how a tank collapsed that morning and five firemen from Cardiff were killed in the resulting blaze. There is not much said that evening.

Alice finds the firemen most polite and considerate while they stay. She is more than happy to feed the men who are trying to save them from further danger. She is also glad of the company during the early afternoon as the days can be long and drag on without any company.

On Saturday morning the fire rages on and a letter arrives from Robert pleading for answers to his questions on their safety. Alice knows he may have received her first letter by now, but not the second that outlines more of the details. The separation of distance is made worse by the separation in time that letter writing brings. She knows his patience is going to be tested to the limit.

Chapter 5

Training

19th August 1940, Lowestoft

Waking early on Monday morning, Robert dresses in his new uniform and inspects himself in the small bathroom mirror to ensure his appearance is smart and that nothing is left to chance. After a simple breakfast, he chooses to walk to Sparrow's Nest, encouraged by the morning sunshine, and happy for the chance to arrive at the base in a positive frame of mind. He focuses his thoughts on making a good first impression and as he walks he plays through several scenarios where he will meet other ratings and officers. Wearing his uniform for the first time, he is very aware of the way it makes him feel, adding to his sense of steadfastness and purpose. Subconsciously, his gait transforms into a march.

Arriving at 0740, Robert uses the extra time to check the notice board for the training schedule and the assignment of ratings to different teams. All recruits are placed in teams based on their previous experience and the recognised skills recorded when they signed up. Robert buys a hot drink from the NAAFI, more to pass the time than anything else, and as he stands quietly he is lost in his thoughts of home and his absence on his son's birthday. This leaves him knotted inside.

At 0800 there is a pause for the Colours ceremony. The general approach for those who do not know any different is to stand to attention as the ensign is raised. Following this important tradition, the morning continues with basic drill instruction. Acknowledging the importance of high standards in the navy, he is resigned to the minimal level of drill instruction that is required every morning for the next two weeks. The broader training schedule is demanding, and all recruits must learn quickly to achieve the standards expected of them. Robert copes with the square bashing as he looks forward to the timetabled sessions where seamanship is the priority. Making the most of what he is told, he cannot avoid making comparisons with the knowledge that has been handed down to him over the years. With his familiarity of the sea, he often believes he is more experienced than those giving the training, but he knows this is a dangerous trap to avoid at all costs. Operating ships is the same wherever you are from, but the challenge here is to detect the specific way the navy want things done. If he is unable to adapt to the navy approach, the navy ranks, and the specific language of commands, then he will struggle during training and he will not get what he most wants, respect from the naval seamen.

The first day of training ends with many tired and hungry men milling around the NAAFI. Despite their tiredness, they are making plans to head for the pubs after their evening meals, but Robert decides not to commit to the drinking at this point and leaves his decision until later.

At this time of the day, Robert is completely unaware of the events that have struck Pembroke Dock.

Tuesday morning arrives and Robert wakes early. He slept reasonably well having turned in early, but he was woken at some point in the night, disturbed by men returning to his digs from the pub. Feeling refreshed he tries to imagine how some of the sore heads will survive the day with drill orders bellowed to take their effect.

Arriving on foot he has just a few minutes before Colours to check the noticeboard. Next to the schedule for the day, he finds a pinned note with his name across the front. Reading it, he learns that he must report to the administration office after the parade. The day's ceremony concludes quickly and there is only a short time available before his first instruction session starts, so he hightails it to the main office and hands the note to the seaman manning the front desk. Immediately, he is invited into an office just off a short corridor, where he is surprised to see Commander Morris sitting at his desk.

'Sir. This is Crawford,' announces the seaman.

'Thank you, Oaks,' replies the Commander, as Robert stands to attention in front of the desk. The office is sparse with a few photographs as the only gesture to decoration.

'Hello, Crawford. How are you settling in?'

'Very good, sir.'

'Good. Well, I've got some good news for you, Crawford. We failed to take your status as a Trawler Skipper into account when you registered on Sunday. Do you have your Skippers Certificate with you?'

'Yes, sir,' replies Robert as he quickly retrieves it from his wallet to show the commander.

'So, we are making you up to Second-Hand.'

'Thank you, sir.'

'I expect you wanted to be a Skipper in the Patrol Service. Well, that will come with time and after you have more experience of the Royal Navy.'

'Very well, sir.'

'We need experienced men like you in the service Crawford. You can make a big difference with the training of the crews, so please recognise this and give us your best.'

'I will sir. Thank you.'

'Carry on.'

Robert tries to leave the room in the smartest manner possible, but in his excitement, he cannot quite pull off the coordination required to turn on the spot and march out of the door. Recognising his promotion as good news, he commits himself to absorb all the training, and he realises he now has his sights set on becoming a Patrol Service Skipper. He has his target.

Plans for a visit to the pub that Tuesday evening are made, and Robert finds it easy to accept as he wants to celebrate his promotion and get to know the recruits better. He is only expecting to be there for a couple of hours.

They have been at the pub a short while and are enjoying their first drink. Sitting next to Robert is John Underhill, a recruit on the same intake team as him. The two men live at the same digs and had struck up a conversation on the short walk over to the pub. Sitting at a small table in the bay window they continue their discussion, and both learn about each other's hometowns. Links to home are a common way for the recruits to make connections with each other and with this as a backdrop Robert interrupts the conversation and reaches over the table to pick up a discarded newspaper. Through all the noise and distractions in the pub, his eyes found and homed in on two words that start a small section at the bottom of the front page. The headline 'Pembroke Dock Oil Tank Fire Rages,' sets his heart pounding through his rib cage. His stomach tightens as he tries to slow himself down so he can read the details. It does not take much for Underhill to notice there is something wrong.

'Is there a problem Robert?'

'I don't know. I'm just reading this report here that says the enemy has bombed the Fuel Storage depot at Pembroke Dock.'

'Isn't that where you live,' comes the unavoidable but regrettable question.

'Yes, that's exactly where I live. Those oil tanks are less than a mile from my house.'

'Oh, I see,' replies John, not knowing what to say.

'It says here that on the 19th August three Junkers JU88s bombers flew up Milford Haven and across Pembroke Dock to drop bombs on the fuel depot. There are no casualties.'

'Well, that's something,' adds John, still struggling to find the right sympathetic words.

'They say many of the tanks are on fire and they have fire brigades from all over Wales attending. The bombs only hit one tank, but it has spread to others. What can I do? My family are there, very close to this. There is a big dip in the land between where I live and the tanks. I live on the other side of the hill to that dip, but it must be very scary for those in the town. What must Alice be thinking?'

'Well, it sounds like there is no immediate danger. Let's go back to the digs and see if we can have a quiet mug of tea and talk it over. Do you think you could get some leave?'

'No, I've only just arrived, and they made me Second-Hand today so I can't leave even if I wanted to. I've got to complete this training. I've got to make this work.'

'Oh, I see. Let's get back to the digs anyway,' suggests John for the second time as he stands and partly manoeuvres Robert through the busy pub, to the door.

Walking without speaking, the two men complete the short walk back to their digs and with no one there to disturb them, they settle down at the table used for breakfast. Following an emotional description of the situation of his home in relation to the oil tanks, Robert retires to his room and tries to write the hardest letter of his life.

Posting the letter is Robert's priority on his walk to the Nest on Wednesday morning. His mind is in conflict, as his irrational thoughts collide with his balanced views. Slowly, he brings them under control as he reaches back through the emotions of the past few days and recognises the attitude and resilience that brought him here in the first place. His determination keeps his worries in check.

Robert immerses himself in the training schedule and eliminates all but the most positive thoughts. The training is intense, and it focuses on three main areas, seamanship, telegraphy, and weaponry.

For Robert, the seamanship side brings together many of the disciplines that trawlermen and navy sailors have in common. Courses on operating the helm, engine maintenance and safety are all important, but Robert focuses his efforts on navigation with the express hope that he can gain an understanding of the navy's expectations.

Men selected for the telegraphy role have the most intense training at the Nest despite the requirement to have had previous experience in this field. The training in the navy for telegraphists is a course that lasts three months. The Morse code tests have rates set for reading and writing that could never be achieved in the limited time spent at the Nest, and for this reason, the RNPS is advertising for volunteers with previous experience and often take them directly from the Royal Naval Reserve.

Weaponry skills are taught on the Naval 12-Pounder practise equipment on site, with the occasional chance to live fire machine guns and rifles at a nearby range. Robert receives minimal weapons training, and he knows this could be problematic when he needs to organise live firing exercises at sea. Loading real rounds and live firing the main gun on board his future ship is not that far away. He hopes he is not at a disadvantage when the time comes.

Training days require hard work. Fatigue does not stop Robert as his first thought at the end of the instruction is to check to see if any post has arrived. On Thursday he receives a letter from Alice that mentions how happy the children are and only goes into brief details of the fire and its effects. Finishing the letter, he knows that they are obviously safe, but he cannot help feeling that important details are missing. He must write this evening and ask for more information.

Investing a lot of time on navigation training, Robert is trying to ensure he is completely familiar with the naval approach, while also keeping busy and not allowing time for worry. He has been navigating his own trawler for years, but he does not want to leave anything to chance. Knowing he does not thrive well in the classroom, he worries about the details he needs to learn and wanting to be a strong navigator he remembers how much he needed to adjust to the local sea conditions when he first moved to Milford.

He comes up with an idea that he wishes he had thought of earlier, especially as his time at the Nest is short. He asks the local instructors if they know of an experienced trawler skipper who has fished the waters off Suffolk. His enquiries quickly lead him to a local trawler skipper who many agree is the recognised expert. Robert arranges to meet the Skipper who is a retired Royal Navy Reserve man.

'Good morning. Are you Skipper White?' inquires Robert, meeting his contact for the first time in the Nest's NAAFI.

'Yes, hello, you must be Robert Crawford. Pleased to meet you.'

'Yes, I'm Robert. Pleased to meet you too. Please take a seat and I'll get some drinks.'

Robert gets them both a cup of tea and they sit down at a table together.

'Thank you for agreeing to meet me. I'm hoping you can help me with some details of the sea off this coast. I'm a trawler skipper and I know speaking to a fellow trawlerman is the best way for me to learn.'

'Well, I'll try. Do you know where you are going to patrol?'

'No, not at the moment. We have not been assigned ships yet, but I know it will be to the south of here based on some conversations I've had. We'll know for definite in a couple of days.'

'That's fine. I can start to give you some pointers that apply to so much of the coast around here.'

'That's good. I'm happy to be talking to someone who has fished around the coast. I know some men know the sea around here but until you have trawled for fish you don't know the subtle depths and tides to watch out for.'

'Yes, trawling tells you a lot. The real problems around here are shifting sandbanks that can catch you out. They don't shift that quickly and many are marked well on the charts with lights and buoys, but at low tide, a simple bank or bar can have only shifted a couple of feet and you will touch bottom.'

'Right, so I need the charts and buoy positions to start with, but I must make sure to watch out at low tide.'

'Yes, there is something else you can use but it isn't easy to pick up and it takes experience.'

'I realise a lot of this is down to experience.'

'Well, the best thing to look for at low tide is the colour of the water. You can often detect the sand below the waves based on the colour of the water, but it depends a lot on the amount of sunlight you have.'

Robert lodges this important piece of advice away as he knows his previous experience is more relevant to deeper waters where there are no sandbanks to negotiate.

'I'll bear that in mind. Thank you for your advice.'

'You are more than welcome. I'm very happy to help anyone willing to go out to face the enemy at this time. We should go to the chart room and there I can give you some more of an idea of what you are up against.'

'That is very good of you,' replies Robert as they head off for an hour in the Nest's chart room. Later the men part and Skipper White makes Robert the offer of working with him again when his ship's patrol location is known.

At the end of Monday of his second week at the Nest, there is another welcome letter from Alice. She goes into much more detail in this letter and explains the visit from the police to all the houses to outline what is happening and to allay their fears. He reads the letter more than once to make sure he has picked up as much detail as he can. He feels the family is not in any immediate danger and he hopes the emergency finishes soon.

Monday's newspapers are full of stories of bombing raids on London and the retaliatory attacks on Berlin. The shift to civilian targets causes shock and anger amongst the men with everyone at the Nest now keen to get to sea to do their duty. The men's bravery hides their concern for their families at home and Robert feels he has a head start on them all.

During the lead up to the declaration of war sections of the east coast of the North Sea have been heavily mined by the British. The mine defence barrier creates protected sea lanes for coastal shipping convoys to carry supplies up and down the country. At specific points in the barrier, there are strategically placed gaps for ships to navigate into the broader North Sea.

During the early stages of the war, the enemy were laying their own new mines in the protected lanes, in the gaps and also close to British ports. Initially, the enemy mines were laid by destroyers and U-Boats that moved freely through the protected lanes and gaps. Continuous sweeping of these areas was required to keep them clear of enemy mines. The RNPS built up its strength to patrol the protected lanes, the gaps and to ensure that the minesweepers were protected as they did their vital work.

In this dangerous environment, ships need careful seamanship and excellent navigation skills to avoid each other and to avoid the man-made dangers created by the mines. Equally importantly, the ships must navigate around the natural dangers of sandbanks, shoals and shifting tides. There is no room for error. The country must be defended at all costs.

The training regime at the Nest is starting to affect levels of concentration and most of the men start to show signs of strain. Everyone is focused on getting assigned to their ships and leaving on patrol. There is a strong sense of duty and honour to carry them through.

In the meantime, there is a small amount of time to relax, make friends and enjoy the pubs, music hall or the town's cinema. These distractions all help to keep their minds off separation from their families and the reality of going to war.

Chapter 6

Crew Attention

31st August 1940, Lowestoft

Training nears completion, and Robert is relieved that the officers are close to announcing the crew and ship allocations. Each man is identified by the service number they received when they first arrived at the Nest and as Robert's service number starts with LT/JX he knows he is allocated out of RNPS for the duration of the war. The "J" indicates he has been recognised as a Seaman and it means a lot to him that his experience has been acknowledged as the "X" puts him on a pay scale that ended in 1925. Together with his promotion to Second Hand, it could make a big difference to the position he is given within the ship's crew when the allocations are announced.

Finally, the day arrives, and expectations are high as the men gather to hear the ships they are assigned to and importantly who else is in their crew. Strong opinions have already formed, and the men know who they want to go to sea with and who they want to avoid. A senior officer calls out the name of a ship and the Skipper for that vessel makes himself known by raising his arm. The crew for that ship are then called out by name and the men start to organise themselves into various groups as they move towards their chosen Skipper. Robert learns he is joining a ship called Caithness, one of His Majesty's Trawlers. The ship was hired by the navy from its Hull based owner earlier in the year. The ship is a trawler that has recently returned from being converted to the role of an Auxiliary Patrol vessel. Robert approves of the Scottish origin of the ships name and he hopes that it is a good omen for them all.

The Skipper of the Caithness stands out based on his uniform and the authority he uses to gather the men together. Taller than Robert, he appears to be close to six feet tall and his physical presence is strong, carrying himself with the confidence of a man who has always been in charge of other men. A peaked cap sits on a head of cropped blond hair and sharp blue eyes look out from underneath the brim, seemingly alert to all around him. A fresh freckled face hints at a fair skin that has had much less exposure to weather erosion than the trawlermen in the vicinity. His immaculate appearance contrasts with the ratings around him and there is a scale of fastidiousness that Robert can measure himself against.

The ship's command has been given to a Royal Naval Reserve man and despite Robert's own experience, he accepts that this was always going to be the way the allocation would work out. Not all is lost, as he is the only Second-Hand in the crew and that puts him directly in command after the Skipper. Based on their uniform, Robert recognises one other

Royal Navy Reserve man in the fifteen-man crew, together with a familiar Royal Navy rating. The remainder of the Caithness crew are men from trawlers and other fishing backgrounds. They introduce themselves to one another in a friendly and relaxed manner that is typical of the RNPS. At this crucial moment, they are all meeting, not for the first time, but for the first occasion with a new identity, that of a ship's crew. Fifteen men are now in this war together.

Their new ship is currently moored up at the harbour in Lowestoft. The crew is told to return to their digs for one more night, before bringing their kit to tomorrow's Colours, ready to board a truck to travel the short distance to the harbour. They are about to start living together on the ship and most of the men know that their accommodation standards are about to drop significantly. Some men have been unfortunate and been given digs that were in a terrible state but for most of the men, this is a great chance to have a decent meal and a restful night's sleep. This is the last night in comfortable beds for many weeks.

While the men talk to each other, Robert approaches the Skipper and asks if he can have a word. 'Of course,' replies Robinson in his broad Cornish accent. 'Good to have you in the crew Crawford. I've looked over your details and I am looking forward to sailing with you.'

'Thank you, Skipper,' replies Robert, as they shake hands firmly. 'How do you want to start with the crew tomorrow?' asks Robert as his way of trying to figure out the Skipper's priorities.

'Let's get aboard tomorrow and work out the duties and watches as you see fit. I'd like to get underway at noon and see how everyone performs together. We are based out of Harwich, and we start patrols on Monday, so we don't have too much time to work through everything. Here's the list of the crew. Please look through it and suggest how you would set up the watches.'

'Thank you, Skipper,' acknowledges Robert as he is handed a typed list of the crew's names.

'Carry on,' comes the reply and the men exchange salutes.

After the discussion, Robert is left unsure how his relationship with his new commanding officer will develop. His first impressions are good, and he recognises authority in the man he has just met. The kind words of welcome are appreciated and there is no doubt that delegation to organise the watches is a sign of trust.

Most trawler Skippers have a fierce reputation and run their ships without compromise. Robert believes he is from a different mould and prefers to lead with firmness and fairness. Robert wants to gain the respect of the men in his charge, and he believes the best way to achieve this is to lead from the front. He never asks a man to do anything he is not prepared to do himself and this has been his guiding principle for leading men aboard his ships and it has held up well for him over many years at sea. While he is not the Skipper of this crew, his role is pivotal and he may need to step around a few things until he finds its natural balance, especially as the Commanding Officer is from a Royal Navy Reserve background. Leadership is full of difficult choices, and it is often lonely, but doing it from the second seat is a new challenge for Robert.

Reading the typed list of names, Robert is struck by the young age of the crew, with many under thirty and some under twenty-five. Considering himself young at the age of thirty-one he also knows that it is his experience that counts, now more than ever. The crew has three stokers and two enginemen to help keep the ship propelled through the water and nine seamen, including himself, to crew the deck and wheelhouse. Immediately, his priority is to work out who has the specialist skills needed to make the two watches work. He must identify wireless telegraphists, those with weapons training and also those who can fill general seamanship roles. Approaching the men who are mingling around him, he manages to talk to each of them and get their particulars.

Robert recognises James Fredricks and is glad to find him in the crew. Remembering back to their meeting in London, he recalls their conversation in the pub when Fredricks explained how he had volunteered from the Royal Navy. Knowing the navy man is trained on weapons is a great help, but he could also be a very useful helmsman due to his excellent training record. He seeks out Fredricks and welcomes him warmly, 'Good to see you again Fredericks. I'm very happy to have a man with your skills aboard. I may need to ask you to help with the men's weapons training and give them more than the basic instruction they have had so far.'

'Good to see you, Crawford. I see you're our second-hand so should I call you sir.'

'No, that's not right. I think the Skipper is the only one you should be calling sir.'

'Ah, I'll try to remember that. Yes, happy to help with any gun training. I'm also trained on the helm, so if I can help with that, I'm your man.'

'Yes, that is a big help. Glad to have you onboard,' repeats Robert before he moves on to talk to the other men gathering nearby.

Speaking briefly to the enginemen and the stokers, he is reassured as he recognises all the skills necessary to run the boiler room and engine room together as a strong unit. Stokers are a breed of men that few understand, with their working conditions indescribable to anyone who has not felt the heat, let alone worked a four-hour watch in the dark and noisy bowls of the ship. Enginemen work their magic with the trawler's steam engines and Robert knows he will count on them heavily as they keep the ship operating night and day.

Working through the list, Robert gets the men to say what they are trained on and how long they have worked at sea. The wireless telegraphist post is covered by the RNR crewman who is already trained on the equipment they will have aboard. Robert needs to find another telegraphist as one specialist must always be available and on watch. Asking if anyone has been trained on the wireless, Robert is relieved as a man named Bowes comes forward, explaining that he has worked with wirelesses all his life and that he has also attended the training courses here at the Nest. The skills of the men are coming together to compliment the whole crew and Robert notices them standing tall as they offer their services. No sign of an obvious cook emerges but that is a problem that will naturally solve itself when the men get to know each other better and the hard, physical work generates a good appetite.

Robert thanks the men for their help, and they disperse, making their own plans to meet for drinks later that evening. He wants to get back to his digs, sort through his kit, and most importantly write a letter home as it has been over a week since his last letter was posted. He has received another letter from Alice, but the oil tank fire is still raging, and his concerns still linger. Hoping he can join them at the pub later, he knows he must invest the time to get to know them in a relaxed way before they head off to sea together.

Returning quickly to his room, Robert swiftly sorts through his kit, but the letter writing proves to be a slow and demanding task. He is motivated to write, and he knows the pleasure of getting a letter in return, but on this occasion, he finds it hard to explain why he has chosen to be away from the family he longs to see. He is conflicted.

With his letter written, he makes his way from his digs to the pub the men have chosen for the night's merriment. The beer is good, and the discussions are in full flow. The men are keen to leave for sea the next day, but they are not destined for an early night. The Skipper has not joined them and noticing this, one of the crew quickly approaches Robert.

'What do you make of the Skipper?' asks one of the Stokers.

'What's your name, lad?' asks Robert.

'John,' replies the young man.

'Well John, he has a lot of experience,' replies Robert, keen not to judge anyone too soon or too harshly, 'and I expect him to lead us into this war with determination and courage.'

'But is he going to be a hard man?', the young man pushes.

'Remember he is the Skipper lad,' Robert replies as he thinks back to his own challenges leading the crew and gaining their respect. 'Let's go to sea and we'll all learn about each other then, yes?' John takes this answer well and knows he should not push any further.

The evening passes pleasantly with the men telling tales of their past adventures, some believable, and others stretching everyone's imagination. Robert has observed this group of men for a few hours, and while it is early days, he is beginning to see them bonding. While this social gathering is important, he must focus on how they will perform onboard. Noticing many of them over the past two weeks, he recognises many of their faces and has spoken to a few of them, but from the moment he was handed that list, they are now part of his crew. He has a great challenge and a great responsibility to lead these men. Together they will succeed.

Robert starts to leave after a few drinks and turns to the men to remind them to be at Colours in the morning, with their full kit, ready to leave. They acknowledge his disguised order, and he feels this is starting to work out well for him.

Sunday is grey and overcast, as the crew ride in a navy truck, travelling the short distance down from the Nest to Lowestoft's outer harbour. Pulling up alongside the converted trawler HMT Caithness, the crew get their first sight of their new ship. The vessel is a ten-year-old steam trawler, requisitioned from its owners over two months ago, and in that time the ship has been fitted with standard armaments and the wireless set has been brought up to navy standards. She is a good-looking trawler with a low deck, masts forward and aft and a large funnel behind the wheelhouse. Robert looks down the length of the ship and realises this is bigger than any trawler he has ever worked on.

The RNPS has three main types of converted trawler under its command. There are Minesweepers used to trawl the sea for mines anchored on the seabed. There are also Anti-Submarine trawlers to detect and locate submerged U-Boats. The third type of converted trawler is configured for Auxiliary Patrol use and is designed to protect shipping channels from airborne attack and surface ship assault. HMT Caithness is configured for this third type of role as an Auxiliary Patrol vessel, and this dictates the type of work the crew can expect.

Climbing out of their truck, the men view their new ship and immediately draw comparisons to the trawlers they have previously served on. The most obvious difference is the imposing 12-Pounder gun now fitted on a raised steel platform in front of the foremast on the foc'sle. The sight of this gun jolts a few of the men into remembering why they are here, while Robert on the other hand realises he has a lot to organise before they can get the ship underway by noon.

'Alright to get the men aboard, Skipper?'

'Yes, Second-Hand,' was the formal reply.

'Aye Sir,' responds Robert making a gesture that the Skipper should be first aboard. The crew follow the Skipper and second-hand up the gangway, but before they start to explore the ship, Robert calls them together to allocate them to their sleeping quarters. Dividing the cabins amongst the crew does not pose any problems as Robert puts himself and the more senior crew in the aft cabin with its six berths. Just below the galley, the aft cabin contains the mess room and most importantly is close to the stern. This is an advantage, because your ability to sleep during a rough sea on a ship of this size, is mainly determined by how close you are to the stern. The more junior crew made up of the ordinary seamen, the enginemen and the stokers are all allocated to the forward cabin. The eight men in this cabin have space to spare, with fifteen berths to choose from, but in comparison, there are no home comforts, and it is bare, apart from a stove to keep them warm. Robert is trying to balance the crew's levels of seniority against a general sense of fairness, and he knows he cannot win. He stops trying after hearing a few complaints and tells the men it has been decided.

With the cabins arranged, Robert hands out instructions to the crew so that they all know the jobs they need to do before they head for sea. 'Enginemen and stokers check out our coal bunkers and prepare the boiler and engine ready to depart. Brown, you take a man and check our general supplies and the amount of freshwater aboard. Locke, look over the wireless room behind the wheelhouse and test that we can talk to HQ. Fredricks, take two men and report back on all the armaments and ammunition aboard. Everyone else, inspect the ship and report any problems back to me. I'll be in the wardroom with the Skipper.'

The men scatter to their tasks as Robert follows the Skipper to the wardroom where they find a well looked after cabin, lined with teak, brass fittings and an upholstered bench seat around a drop-leaf table.

Robert is asked to take a seat.

'She's ten years old but looks in good nick. I hope she's mechanically sound and up to the job we need her to do.'

'We'll know soon enough sir. I'm sure the crew will find anything that's wrong. The journey to Harwich will tell us a lot. Here's my work on the crew list and on the back I've divided the crew into two teams to secure the watches.'

Watches are a system of time slots that have been used on ships for centuries, with the aim of manning important areas at all times of the day and night.

The watch system divides the twenty-four-hour day into six sections, each four hours long. From 2000 hours the First, Middle and Morning watches take you through a twelve-hour stretch to 0800 hours. The Forenoon and Afternoon watches are simply named and take you round to 1600 hours. The remaining four hours of the day, up to 2000 hours, are called the Dog watch. This final watch is split into two, so everyone switches their allocation each day.

The Caithness is a small ship, and the crew size is at the limit of the number needed to man it effectively. The crew must be divided into two so there is an equal number of men working a given watch, while a similar number are resting or asleep.

The ship's bell marks out each half-hour of time, resulting in four rings of the bell for the midpoint and eight bells for the end of a watch.

Robert has done his homework and wants to impress the Skipper. During the previous evening, he has worked on the teams and watches and written the outcome on the back of the crew list he was given. The challenge was ensuring the availability of two fully functional teams across the watch pattern. Mapping out the skills he ensures he has a telegraphist, helmsman, lookout, engineman, one stoker, cook and leader on each of the watches. As a crew of fifteen, they have a minimal team of seven roles and there is no room for sickness or injury. Robert believes this is too tight to run the ship safely and to add to his challenge he must make the whole crew available to transition to action stations. He allocates five crew to man the main gun and two others to man the Lewis guns. His problem is that gunners cannot come from the main watch crew on duty, as wireless, helm and other tasks still need to run uninterrupted while the guns are manned. Robert devises a team list with the main role for each man on watch and also assigns each one an additional "action stations" role if they are not on watch. Pleased with the simple plan, he knows that most men need many more hours of experience to make it work well.

'Very good,' says the Skipper, adding, 'who's leading the watches?'

'That's you and me Skipper and then Locke if we need him, as he's the most experienced coming from the Royal Naval Reserve.'

'Very good,' says the Skipper again, adding, 'we'll have all hands take the ship down to Harwich. I'd like to see how everyone works the ship and there are also some minor drills I'd like to check through on the way. I'll plot a course down so we should meet in the wheelhouse twenty minutes before we sail. Carry on Crawford.'

'Aye, sir' replies Robert as they both stand, and he remembers to salute.

Climbing the ladder on the port side of the wheelhouse, Robert steps onto the walkway, an elevated section of decking that surrounds the wheelhouse on three sides. A metal handrail gives limited protection from falling in heavy seas and a Lewis gun mount is positioned at each of the front corner positions. The raised wheelhouse walkway is the best vantage position aboard, and Robert plans to post the watch lookout there when underway. Robert decides to refer to the walkway as the "bridge" in future as he does not want the men to confuse it with the wheelhouse itself. Both places can get busy when action stations are called, and he prefers precise and distinct names to guide operations.

Taking in a full view of the ship he is satisfied with the work he has set in progress and returning to the port door of the wheelhouse he enters another teak panelled room, sat in its prominent position amidships. He familiarises himself with the layout, noting the wireless room access through its connecting door where Locke is working away at the recently installed equipment.

Returning to deck level, he takes a quick tour of the ship from bow to stern. Checking in on the forward cabin and working towards the stern he takes in the boiler room, engine room, galley, and aft cabin. He stops to talk to the crew as he goes, telling each of them their team allocation and offering encouragement to each man as they ask questions. The queries are designed to check him out rather than to seek clarity for any real problems. Everyone is trying to get the measure of everybody else aboard ship.

At 1140 hours, Robert joins the Skipper in the wheelhouse.

'Ah, good, are we ready Crawford?.

'Yes, sir. The boilers have been fired, we have confirmed wireless contact with Harwich, there are plenty of supplies aboard, including enough coal for our upcoming patrol but food supplies need improving.'

'Good. I have a course plotted which will take us the forty-eight nautical miles to Harwich. This ship is capable of ten knots, so we can steam at a steady full speed and get there by 1700 hours. We can then moor up, secure the ship and all eat at the start of the second dog watch. Carry on Crawford.'

'Aye, sir.'

Robert has already briefed the crew on leaving harbour, so everyone is ready above and below decks. The boiler has been fired since the moment they joined the ship, and the engine has been given a thorough check. Orders to cast off all lines are given, and the Skipper uses the engine telegraph to instruct the engine room to go dead slow ahead. Harbourside ratings help release the mooring lines and the ship gets underway. A large amount of smoke is generated from the boiler and the steel hull shudders into life as the engine, driveshaft and screw connect to churn up the water. The wheelhouse is manned by the Skipper, Stanford at the helm and Robert overseeing the actions of the crew. The Skipper is giving the helmsman simple instructions to leave the harbour and head for the sea. As they get underway, the speed is increased via the engine telegraph to half ahead, and Robert has his eyes everywhere as he checks on the way the ship runs through the water and the state of the crew as they man a completely unfamiliar vessel. All is going well, as various shouts across the deck help organise activities, and the crew give their very best to make this inaugural journey start with a sense of pride.

The sea is slight, the wind is a force three north-easterly and visibility is good. The sky is still grey, but the conditions are ideal for taking a ship to sea for the first time. When the ship is two miles off the coast the Skipper gives the order, 'come right to one-nine-zero'.

The helmsman replies, 'Come right to one-nine-zero, Aye, aye sir.'

The helmsman moves the wheel and reports the manoeuvre with the response, 'Steady on course sir.'

'Very well,' responds the Skipper as he gives a new instruction via the engine telegraph, full ahead, and the engine room acknowledges the change of speed by moving their side of the telegraph to full ahead.

'We'll steam at ten knots on this course until we see Orfordness lighthouse, on the coast. Then we'll turn right onto course two-three-zero and this will take us to Harwich. This is a swept shipping lane and according to Harwich, there are no new reports of mines in this area. However, we should keep an extra lookout, post someone on the bridge Crawford.'

'Aye, sir. We'll carry on with my watch team and change for the first dog watch at 1600,' replies Crawford as he knows the Skipper will want to bring the ship into Harwich Harbour.

'Crawford, I'll be in the wardroom if I'm needed. Carry on'.

'Aye sir,' answers Robert as he wonders if he will ever get used to the Royal Navy commands and the formality used by the Skipper. Accepting he is in a pivotal role, he needs to link the navy ways to the approach the men expect to see on a trawler. He knows it is a sound and accepted way of working, so he must adapt and from the bridge, he tells the crew visible on deck that he is leading the watch and his team need to man their positions. Robert tells the men to pass on his message and inform the rest of the crew to be ready for the first dog watch.

Robert posts Slater to the lookout on the bridge. Giving Slater a good set of binoculars, he tells him to report anything he sees on the sea or anything else for that matter. It is reasonable to assume that at this time of day, and on this course, they will not encounter anything, but everyone remembers the training messages of vigilance and alertness.

A focus on the dangers of their journey does not stop Robert from taking in the seascape and the lay of the coast off their starboard side. There is a single large stretch of stony and sandy beach, stretching for tens of miles, as they pass the coastal towns of Southwold and Aldeburgh. Robert has heard of these places but has never visited the seaside resorts or seen the flat landscape that stretches into the distance behind the coast. Many rivers approach the sea from inland, but first, take parallel paths to the beaches. The River Ore follows this type of course and Robert marvels at its beauty and contrasts it to the stretches of water he knows off the coasts of Scotland and West Wales.

With Slater on lookout and his own watch in the wheelhouse, Robert leans out of the door and gives instructions to a crewman as he passes. 'Bowes isn't it,' he enquires.

'Aye,' comes the acknowledgement.

'Go down to the engine room and ask one of the enginemen to come to the wheelhouse?'

'Aye,' says Bowes and immediately heads down to the engine room to pass on the second-hand's request.

Robert is back in the wheelhouse when he is joined by Thomas, the senior of the two enginemen, easily identifiable by his oil-streaked overalls. They talk at length about the state of the ship's boilers and engines, both trying to work out between them if they are likely to have any problems. Thomas has lots of experience with the design of this ship's triple-expansion engine as it is a type used for many years in trawlers and small ships. Talking freely, they get to know each other for a short while before Thomas returns to the engine room. Robert believes the engineman is going to be a great asset and he is sure he will keep the ship running smoothly whatever the conditions.

Robert rings eight bells from the front of the bridge and waits for the Skipper and his watch crew to join them in the wheelhouse. The crew not on the first dog watch take themselves off to their cabins to get a hot drink and catch up on some sleep. Before Robert leaves, he and the Skipper get a chance to inform each other of what they have learnt over the past few hours and Robert gives a good account of the crew before handing over to the Skipper to change course as they approach the Orfordness lighthouse.

Sitting in the aft cabin, Robert drinks his mug of tea and chats to Fred Slater who he had talked to earlier in the day while he had been lookout on the bridge. They discover from each other where they had worked before the war and it is easy for them to talk to each other given their shared experiences. As the talking continues the ship's engine note suddenly dies. Both men utter some exclamations and rush to the ladder from the aft cabin and out of the galley onto the main deck. Robert gets to the ladder at the base of the wardroom and climbs, only to be met by the Skipper standing on the bridge.

'Crawford, we've lost steering, so I cut power and we're slowing to a stop.'

'What happened sir?'

'I gave Fredricks instructions to change our course at the lighthouse, but he couldn't move the wheel.'

Robert makes his way into the wheelhouse and greets Fredricks, saying, 'what's happened?'

'I started to turn the wheel, there was some shuddering and then it wouldn't budge'.

Robert steps to the wheel and gives it a turn to the left and then the right but there is no movement. 'Right, that's well and truly stuck. Must be the steam gear. Where is it?'

The men look at each other and work out quickly that the wheel shaft passes under the floor and back through the wheelhouse rear wall. They move to the door on the port side of the back wall of the wheelhouse and find the location of the steering gear between the wheelhouse and the wireless room. This starts to look familiar to Robert as he lifts the false wooden floor and checks the chains running out on the port and starboard side. He knows that this type of set-up has chains running down the side of the wheelhouse, through pullies at deck level and then aft through steering channels to the rudder head arms. The gear room is full of steam and Robert sends Slater off to check the chains to see if anything is fowling them. The Skipper returns to the wheelhouse to check on the ship's course and to check that the lookout on the bridge is still concentrating on the sea ahead of them.

Robert starts to inspect the steam steering gear and very quickly sees that the pipe carrying steam from the boiler has come away from the piston that provides the power to the steering gear. Shutting a value to cut off the steam, he can see where the pipe has separated. Robert goes down to the forward cabin to find Thomas, the senior engineman, as he is the closest crew member they have aboard to a steamfitter. Thomas jumps to life and heads off to find his tools and then look at the job. Robert is keen to check their position with the Skipper, but they have not drifted far on this relatively calm day, although the wind is freshening, and it could edge more towards a force four. As the wind is coming from the northeast it is pushing them slightly towards the shore, but so far this does not concern Robert. The time it takes Thomas to repair the steering gear is the crucial thing and Robert goes to check how things are progressing, desperately trying not to put any pressure on the engineman. Thomas sounds confident he can fix the gear and gives Robert a guess of twenty minutes to be back up and running. Returning to discuss this with the Skipper, Robert suggests contingency plans to reduce their drift, including steaming the ship astern if necessary. Both are concerned about any alteration in the wind direction as a change from the northeast to the northwest will push them off the coast and closer to sandbanks and the infamous mine barrier.

A nervous twenty-five minutes pass before Thomas reports the fix is made and that he needs to test the steering. Robert moves the wheel to port and then starboard and it is free. They get underway again with the Skipper correcting the course to bring them into Harwich. The delay has cost them forty minutes in all and as they approach the harbour, they are surprised by the number of ships entering and leaving the port. Telegraphed signals instruct them to avoid a destroyer that has overtaken them and is now entering the harbour ahead of them.

The entrance to the harbour is guarded by a spur of land on the righthand side. The angle of approach requires the trawler to travel south until they are past the spur and then make a turn to head north and approach Harwich. Their first view of Harwich shows the town on their port side and the men take interest in what will be their new home for the foreseeable future. The Skipper is familiar with Harwich and knows that they are not docking alongside this characterful old town on their left. Passing the harbour entrance there is a headland directly ahead with the River Orwell on the right stretching away into the distance as it continues upstream to Ipswich and beyond. To the left of the headland is the River Stour with a large basin that acts as a harbour and mooring for a large number of ships. The crew marvel at this picturesque and natural stretch of waterway and feel it will make an excellent base for their patrols.

The Caithness steams at a slow pace in the direction of the Stour, aiming for a stretch of land on the southern bank of the river. Their destination is HMS Badger, based at Parkeston Quay. The RNPS has a shore station there with the facilities needed to berth and supply many ships. It is the HQ and operations base for a broader Navy command and has many hundreds of shore staff.

By 1900 hours they are halfway through the Second Dog watch and arrive alongside to moor up. After securing the ship they gather to eat in the aft cabin and mess room. To Robert, the crew appear happy as he tells them the watch pattern while they are in the port. The watches overnight only require someone to be overseeing the ship from the wheelhouse and to take any signal messages. They plan to go to sea at 0800 hours the following day, so most of the crew stay aboard and drink some rum, while a handful of men cannot resist a visit to the pubs closest to the quay, based in the village of Parkeston. The next patrol is five days long, so for some, a run ashore is essential.

Reflecting on the incident with the steering gear, Robert hopes this is just the typical type of running repair that is often needed at sea. Seafarers are very superstitious so he hopes his more practical view of events will win the day.

Chapter 7

First Patrol

1st September 1940, Harwich

Sunday morning greets the crew with a sky that is turning grey and overcast. Leaving port at 0800 hours, team two takes the ship's forenoon watch, with Robert leading from the wheelhouse. The Caithness is followed by three other converted trawlers and together they make up a patrol group. Each patrol has a designated group officer, and that position is filled by the most senior skipper available, and on this occasion, it is Lieutenant Waldon from HMT Nevern. Receiving orders from Harwich Auxiliary Patrol Operations, the group's duty is to patrol several sectors in the North Sea and report on all sightings of enemy ships, mines, and U-boats.

The RNPS Harwich Command station covers an area from the River Blackwater in Essex and extends to the north near the Suffolk town of Dunwich. Protection of this sea area requires a huge coordination effort and the key to this is the Royal Navy's command-and-control structure developed from years of experience. Operational signals are sent via wireless links from three sub-stations under the overall command of HMS Badger, based in Harwich.

Patrol ships must know that safe sea areas have been swept and cleared of mines. The navigation challenges extend beyond these safe areas and require all patrol craft to know the location of all navy and merchant ships operating in the area. Lookouts are posted for far sightings on the horizon, and near sightings closer to the ship. Larger navy vessels have multiple lookouts that cover different angles, plus any dangers from the air, but smaller ships can only provide one posted lookout with the additional eyes of the helmsman and watch leader.

British minesweepers are mostly converted fishing trawlers and they form a magnificent sight as they steam in formation through the water trawling for mines. The biggest risk to any British ship in the North Sea is the enemy mines currently being laid by destroyers and U-Boats. Enemy destroyers are laying mines very close to the coast and minesweepers are fighting a constant battle to keep convey supply routes open. Enemy vessels appear to have a free run of the swept shipping lanes and many at the highest level of the navy are concerned that this will lead to the disruption or delay of vital supply conveys. Auxiliary Patrol vessels are ordered to support operating minesweepers, report on all coastal activity, and engage enemy vessels when possible.

Robert and the Skipper discuss the dangers they face and realising how unprepared they are for any encounter with the enemy, they agree to prioritise weapons drills during the early days of the patrol. To keep on top of their protection they need men with weapons experience to help build the confidence and skills of the men from fishing backgrounds. An opportunity soon arises, as their patrol area is two hours travel from Harwich, affording the Skipper the chance to involve the whole crew and expose them to action stations.

Knowing he does not have much time, Robert acts swiftly and leaves the wheelhouse to speak to each of the crew to ensure they know their post when the call for action stations is given. Hoping to avoid confusion he takes time to note each man's trained position and compares that to the role they have been selected for onboard. He knows how easy it is for the men to revert to the role they know best rather than one they have been selected to perform and his tally is there to help him check for mistakes. Robert hurries to complete his rounds, as the Skipper's plan may involve trying to catch him out. He is checking with the men off watch in the forward cabin when the ship's bell rings continuously to call all hands to action stations.

From all over the ship, men run to their stations and assume the roles they have been selected to perform. Team two is currently on watch and Robert knows he would normally be in the wheelhouse if he had not been relieved by the Skipper to arrange the drill. With some frustration and annoyance, he makes his way to the wheelhouse, joining the helmsman and the Skipper as he continues to observe the movement of the crew as best as he can.

Locke is already in the wireless room, Slater remains on the bridge as the lookout, while five men speed their way to the foc'sle to man the main 12-Pounder gun. Arranging the weapons cover was Robert's biggest challenge, as he could only rely on men who have received naval gun training while at the Nest. Hall had that training and was a natural choice, however, as an engineman, he may be down in the engine room when called to action stations. There was no way around the problem other than for Hall to always man the gun and for Thomas to head straight to the engine room to cover for him. Robert sees an additional benefit to this arrangement, as he will always have the most experienced engineman in the engine room during action stations. Robert knows the plan is balanced but he is also very aware that it lacks the flexibility needed if men become injured. Robert expects to lose sleep over this situation and feels caught between the need to arm the ship effectively and the need to have men in reserve. Knowing the crew is light on numbers, he accepts this as a national problem and realises he cannot protest to the Skipper. Complaining is not the right thing to do at the start of their first patrol.

Harris and Fredricks bring the Lewis guns from their store behind the wheelhouse and attach them to the mounts at the corners of the bridge. These men are assigned to the Lewis guns from watch team one, while Stanford and Slater are assigned from watch team two. Robert trusts his logic as these men are experienced on the bridge and they are also familiar with the operation of the wheelhouse. Fredricks is the prime gunnery expert, and he has been asked to train the other three men who are already trusted with the responsible positions of helmsman and lookout. The boiler room is manned by two stokers during action stations as this maintains the ship's boiler pressure at this critical time. The ship's speed and manoeuvrability are not the greatest, but both are still crucial at the time of an attack.

The Skipper moves to the front of the bridge and orders the men to load the 12-Pounder with a reduced practise charge and basic ammunition. They are told to aim for a practice target coming up, broad on the starboard bow. Sitting behind the gun's protective steel shield, two gunners are controlling the aiming and the firing of the gun. Behind the gunners stand three men, who load and unload the gun as quickly as possible. The smooth operation of the main gun is essential to the effectiveness of the patrol ship and the five men must drill themselves as often as they can to improve their efficiency.

The Skipper gives the order to fire and there is a flash from the muzzle, followed by a cacophony of sound, and a little later a splash a few hundred yards off the starboard side. Happy with their efforts, the gun crew look to the Skipper for approval. Having practised in different teams while ashore, this is the first time they have worked together, and for the first time, it feels very different, very real, and much more meaningful. The Skipper is aware that Royal

Navy crews can achieve high firing rates on this type of gun, but he is sensible enough to realise that this performance is a world away from what he can expect from these new recruits. The Skipper praises the crew's effort, but Robert sees a reluctance that concerns him.

'Reload,' orders the Skipper and the gun crew ejects the spent case and loads a new projectile and cartridge into the gun. The breech is closed.

'Target two points off the starboard side, fire when ready,' comes the command and the men reposition the gun to its new target and fire. The outcome is the same as before and the gun crew remain satisfied with their efforts.

'Well done', repeats the Skipper. 'Crawford, have the Lewis guns test fired from both sides of the bridge.'

'Aye, sir,' replies Robert before giving the order for the port gun to be test fired into the sea, a short distance from the ship. He warns the gunners to make sure they avoid shooting at the rigging, or any other parts of the ship, as it is all too easy to swing the guns around and lose track of what is around you when you are focussing on a distant target. Robert follows up with the same drill on the starboard side and reports their success back to the Skipper.

'Lewis gun drills finished, sir.'

'Thank you, Crawford. That makes me feel a lot better about the crew's ability to man the guns. We've got depth charges to use on U-Boats, but we don't have any to practice with. Run the crew through the depth settings and how to roll them off the racks at the stern. Once that is completed we can stand down from action stations.'

'Aye, sir,' replies Robert before taking the gun crew aft. Realising he will have to assign two crewmen to the depth charges if the need arises, he feels it is important for them all to run through the drill together. Robert shows the men how to set the hydrostatic pistols for the correct depth of detonation and how to manage the release of one barrel-shaped charge from the angled rack. All the men take note of what is happening and soon Robert is comfortable to call the hands back to their main duties.

Robert pulls Fredericks to one side and asks, 'what did you make of the gun practise earlier?'

'Well, it was good for the first time on the ship, and everyone seemed to know their place.'

'Good, yet I sense a "but" coming.'

'Well, it's currently daylight, the sea is fairly calm, and you aren't trying to hit a moving target that is firing back at you,' comes the sombre response from Fredericks.

'Fine, I'll take that and use it to work with, but I'm going to need your help with this. We need the men working better and more effectively and we have to be able to hit and disable the enemy.'

Fredericks looks Robert squarely in the eye and says, 'I hear you. Just get me the practise time with the men and I'll do what I can.'

'I'll try my best,' answers Robert and the two men part, each knowing things will get serious. Both are happy to trust each other and work together. Fredricks knows his experience will need to work its way through to the men, while Robert believes the men have not yet realised what is being asked of them, especially when the enemy is there for real.

Hearing four bells, the crew acknowledge the halfway point of the forenoon watch as they approach their patrol area for the first time.

After the forenoon watch, Robert takes a cup of tea to the stern and stands to take in the beauty of this area of coastline. He saw it for the first time on their maiden journey to Harwich, but today he is seeing the endless stretch of beaches delicately define the area's signature shoreline. Today's light is emphasising the detail across his boundlessly wide view with many seabirds appearing as the only detectable movement. The peace and tranquillity of the vista is so far removed from his familiar deep sea fishing trips, and it appears to him as a model of calm. Turning the other way, he looks towards the starboard side and across the short expanse of sea. That way lies danger, terror and war.

There are many risks to shipping in the North Sea, and in 1940 the dangers are made many times worse by the use of mines. The East Coast Mine Barrier is a substantial field of British laid mines stretching from the Thames Estuary to the east coast of Scotland. Designed to create a safe shipping lane between itself and the coastline, the barrier prevents enemy vessels from reaching the British cargo convoys, the coastline, and the home ports. The safe shipping lane is divided into many sections, and the one of interest to the Caithness extends from Southend to Yarmouth. It is designated "QZS 148", where the letters "QZ" indicate a mined area, but the addition of the letter "S" indicates it is a "swept" area and therefore safe for merchant and navy vessels.

There are planned gaps in the mine barrier, allowing ships to travel between the safe shipping lanes close to the coast and the rest of the North Sea to the east. The gap in the "QZA 148" region of the barrier, Gap E, is bounded by the Shipwash lightship in the south and the Aldeburgh lightship in the north. Gap E is regularly swept for mines, and vessels from both sides of the conflict can pass through it in relative safety. The gap and the shipping lanes need to be patrolled and today that duty falls to the Caithness and the other vessels in their patrol group. Enemy ships that pass through Gap E, and travel north, will come into direct contact with the Caithness and her patrol.

As well as British mines in this area, there are a vast number of mines being laid by enemy destroyers as they pass through the gaps in the barrier and move freely in the safe shipping lanes to drop their own deadly payload. U-Boats also lay mines inside the safe shipping lanes by defying the barrier and the protection it offers. Mines are ever-present and minesweeping is a constant and dangerous activity. The Caithness joins other auxiliary patrol vessels to combine their efforts between protecting minesweepers and performing their own surface defence and attack role.

The Caithness is assigned a sector within a four-sector pattern, patrolling from the Aldeburgh lightship to a point just north of Dunwich. The patrol ships organise themselves over a chain of sectors, with each sector ten nautical miles in length. Travelling back and forth over its sector, each vessel is closest to another ship at the northernmost and southernmost points of the journey. Passing through waters that have recently been swept for mines, the whole pattern is designed to maximise the chance of detecting and destroying enemy ships as they approach the coastal ports. With a lookout posted on the bridge and the watch leader in the wheelhouse, there is a constant scan of the sea, looking for any activity that might hint of an enemy attack. Repeating their patrol sector day and night, the full line of four ships creates a thin wall of protection between the convoy vessels and the enemy craft that prey on them.

Robert wishes he had another chance to speak to Skipper White, as the experienced trawlerman would be a great help in these waters. When the two men met at the Nest Robert did not know their planned patrol sector, so they talked in general about the sea off the Suffolk coast. Knowing there is no longer a chance to talk, he thinks back to their conversation and draws what he can from the details he can remember.

The crew have had a successful time together during their first day at sea when the telegraph carries a signal with news of further attacks on RAF infrastructure in the South East. The signal warns of increasing air attacks as four hundred and fifty bombers carry out their deadly raids during the day with the loss of life and destruction of airfields happening ninety miles from their current location. Now that they are on active service they feel the impact harder than before. Around the ship, the talk is a mixture of sadness, anger, and concern for the escalating situation.

The crew go about their watch duties or return to their cabins and continue to mull over what this day has brought. It is their first day of active duty and the trawlermen and navy reservists are left in no doubt of the struggle they face.

The sea grows to moderate, with a force five north-easterly wind livening up the conditions, as the day grows steadily warmer and sunnier. It is now halfway through the first dog watch and below deck much of the ship's off duty activity gathers around the galley and the mess room located in the aft cabin. A good supply of tea or cocoa is the attraction, but it is also the only place onboard for the men to sit, chat and get to know each other better. The crew are all young but know the sea better than many their age. Those who have worked on trawlers also know the watch pattern is a tried and tested way to run a ship or trawler at sea. Robert is grateful that the crew have fitted into the system without complaint as that is one less thing for him to worry about.

Robert is concerned about the success of cooking on board with the main meal of the day organised around the changeover between the two dog watches. The food is basic, but the hungry crew have worked hard and have fresh sea air to stoke their appetites. Those about to go on watch eat first before they relieve the current watch, allowing them to have their meal. Cooking onboard a ship is often seen as a punishment, for both the cooks and the crew. However, in all his years at sea, Robert knows there has never been such a good find as Harold James. Known as the man who sailed through weaponry training at the Nest, James already has a crucial role in the crew, but when he offered his services as a cook, Robert smiled and shook him by the hand. James is a rare find, as he enjoys cooking and turns out to be very good at it. William Brown is the other volunteer cook based on his experience cooking on trawlers and with this arrangement Robert feels he has a full crew. Cooked food is a precious commodity, and everyone appreciates the job the cooks do to feed them. Eating on board is a careful process of balance and reaction, as the ship rides the waves, but hungry men start their meal as if it is the first food they have had in days. Their first meal on the first evening on patrol is a great chance for the men to get used to each other and to set expectations for the next five nights at sea. The men appear happy.

By nightfall, the crew have settled into the pattern of watches and at midnight, the first watch makes way for the middle watch and Robert makes straight for the aft cabin to rest before his next duty in four hours. He is just settling down to sleep when the ship's bell rings continuously to call all hands to action stations. Arriving in the wheelhouse with his heart pounding, Robert joins the skipper at the right front window where he is indicating three points to starboard.

'There's a fast-moving craft on a parallel course some twelve hundred yards off the starboard side. Do you see it, Crawford?'

'Let me see,' replies Robert as he takes a pair of binoculars and looks out into the darkness. 'I can't see a flag, but I don't think it's one of ours. I don't recognise the type. Have any enemy sightings come over the telegraph, sir?'

'No. I've asked Bowes to signal the rest of the patrol to see if they have seen anything, but the replies so far say nothing.'

Robert focuses on what he thinks is the wake of the fast-moving craft and says, 'Do you think it's a Destroyer, sir?'

'Yes. It's moving fast and probably more than thirty knots?'

'The gun crew need to stay alert in case it changes course and comes close,' adds Robert as both men search for any sign of alteration in the course of the enemy craft.

'Slowing to half ahead,' shouts the Skipper as he operates the engine room telegraph and returns to scan the darkness. Continuing at high speed, the destroyer starts pulling away from the trawler and the coast.

'So that's the enemy up close,' adds Robert. 'We should signal that to F.O.I.C. Harwich and tell the rest of the patrol group to keep an eye out for it. Maybe one of our destroyers can intercept it.'

'Yes,' agrees the Skipper. 'We can stand down the crew and go back to the watches. We can talk again at eight bells.'

The Skipper shouts, 'stand down hands, full ahead,' as the engine room telegraph is moved to indicate the new speed, followed by an acknowledgement from the men below.

'Aye, sir,' replies Robert as he leaves the wheelhouse and calls to the men to stand down from the 12-Pounder and the Lewis guns. The ship returns to its state of normal watches and Robert makes a note to talk to Fredericks in case either of them knows of a way to improve the action stations call. Robert has concerns about the way the men are struggling to use the wheelhouse ladders at the crucial time. He feels there may be a simpler way to get the guns manned as that must be the priority for the crew. Deciding it can wait, he heads for his berth and the hope of some sleep.

Waking as if no time has passed, he moves to the wheelhouse alongside other crew members changing their watch duties. Thinking back to last night's sighting of the destroyer he is outraged by the proximity of the enemy and catches himself thinking less like a trawlerman and more like the skipper of a warship.

The thought jolts him as he focuses on leading the morning watch. He has decided to lead the ship as best as he can, to ensure the enemy cannot take control of the shipping lanes, and to protect everyone at home. The sea is his life and as second-hand he finds himself in an important position. Despite their short time together, he believes he can trust the crew to do a good job as they man the different parts of the ship. For himself, he must manage the routine of the patrol, keep the Skipper informed and follow his commands, while his sense of loneliness and separation from his family may show through. He recognises others in the crew are having the same feelings, but he chooses to see beyond his own personal fears and is determined to protect the country from the threats it faces. He elects to use this higher purpose as his driving force during the days and months ahead.

Dawn on Wednesday morning appears while Robert is on watch and he greets the new day as a blessing while he occupies a solitary position at the stern of the ship. Finishing his middle watch at 0400 hours, he took the chance to sleep for a couple of hours, before rising for an early breakfast and a hot drink.

It is close to his next watch at 0800 and he is suddenly carried back to Pembroke Dock as he sees a vivid picture of his children in his mind's eye. They are having their breakfast around the kitchen table and the normal everyday scene is such a joy to behold. The eldest children are readying themselves for school as the new term started this week. He imagines the excitement on their faces and thinks of how James is making the most of his mother's attention.

The vision in his head shifts to a different perspective and he sees Alice standing at the window looking out towards the sky. His greatest wish would be to be with them at just that moment. He worries about them and just feels helpless to protect them from the opposite side of the country. He might as well be on the other side of the earth for all the good he can do. He is hit hard by this emotional and poignant connection to home.

Back in Pembroke Dock Alice is busy getting the children ready for the day and preparing to leave the house for the short walk to school. Breakfast is nearly over, and she reminds herself to write to Robert when she returns as he must have gone to sea by now and would welcome a letter on his return to shore.

Wondering if today is destined to follow the same pattern as the day before, Robert reflects on their unremarkable second day on patrol and how the watches flowed into one another. The current forenoon watch is passing without incident and the challenges of the first night start to fade in the memory. The ship is building its routine and the men are carrying out their duties with confidence, even allowing time to run out baited lines to catch fresh fish for their evening meal.

The afternoon arrives and Robert is in the wheelhouse scanning the sea through a set of binoculars that have an image quality better than any he has experienced before. Navy issue binoculars are impressive and their importance at sea easily justifies their quality and expense. Slater is the lookout posted on the bridge and he has the dubious honour of a more bracing watch than those in the sheltered wheelhouse. Slater taps at the window to attract Robert's attention and succeeds as the second-hand turns to see him pointing to something off the port bow. Joining Slater outside, Robert starts to look at whatever is causing the excitement.

'What is it?'

'I don't know, but could it be a mine?', comes the worrying reply, as Slater points to an object floating a couple of hundred yards away, one point to port.

'I think you're right!', exclaims Robert as he immediately reaches for the ships bell attached to the front of the wheelhouse and rings it loudly and continuously to sound action stations. Returning to the wheelhouse, he gives the order to the engine room to continue dead-slow ahead.

'Come right standard rudder,' orders Robert.

'Aye, right standard rudder, responds the helmsman as the Skipper comes through the door to the wheelhouse. Following a quick explanation of what is happening, the Skipper and Robert join Slater on the bridge where they all stare at the mine as the ship slows and turns so the deadly object starts to appear broad on the port side. Commands are given to stop the engine and to set the gun crews to be ready to respond to any enemy action while they are not under power.

Training manuals and current instructions require them to shoot at the mine to sink it to the seabed and avoid detonating the mine on the surface as the explosion is large, unpredictable and likely to shower the ship with mine fragments. Normally, this type of mine is attached to a mooring on the seabed with a length of chain designed to keep it below the surface. In this case, the chain or some part of the mooring has broken, and the explosive buoyant shell is now floating on the surface. Robert feels the mine is taunting them, but he quickly calms himself and calls the two Lewis gunners to report to him with the Lee Enfield rifles stored in the locker behind the wheelhouse.

'Right, let's sink this mine. Can you shoot it from here, Harris?'

'Not at this distance. I think we'll have to get closer. I can't see us hitting it on this sea from much over a hundred yards away.'

'Right, we'll need to steam past it as slowly as we can and try to maintain that distance while you line up on deck. I'll get the helmsman to manage that approach and then come back to join you.'

Robert disappears off to the wheelhouse to explain his plan. The Skipper agrees to manage the helm and engine room, allowing them to keep the required distance between the ship and the mine. Returning to the deck, Robert joins the gunners and watches apprehensively as the ship begins to manoeuvre into position, running a course past the mine. The gunners watch carefully as the ship makes its progress to a point where they can open fire. As they raise their guns to take aim, they adjust to the swell, but it is making it very difficult to hold still despite wanting to get this job done on the first pass. Both men were called out during training for being good shots, and with the ship's crew watching, they put themselves under a lot of pressure. With rifles loaded with ten .303 rounds, both men are ready to fire when given the command. Robert checks their distance from the mine and gives the order to fire. Each man takes aim and fires at the floating target. As Robert watches, the men continually adjust the height of their rifles as they need to compensate for the swell. Twenty rounds later the mine remains floating on the surface, intact and still a danger to all of them. Quickly returning to the wheelhouse, Robert asks the Skipper to turn the ship and make another return pass while the gunners reload their rifles from two chargers they have in their pockets.

The return pass begins, and everyone recognises that the distance has been shortened this time to help the riflemen with their accuracy. Robert returns to the deck and stands with the gunners who are waiting for his command to begin firing. A little while passes and Robert gives the order. Three rounds are fired before a fourth hits the mine, not puncturing the shell, but instead hitting one of the horns that protrude from the case and act as contact triggers. The resulting explosion is gigantic, deafening and accompanied by a shockwave that hits the men in their chests, causing them to stagger. A plume of water shoots high into the air and spreads out to soak the men as it falls. The water is not the only thing falling, as fragments of the mine rain down on the deck, luckily not big enough to cause any serious harm. The men on the deck are frozen to the spot as they take in the explosion, while the men in the wheelhouse rush out to check everyone is unharmed. It is easy to read the shock on everyone' faces as the order to stand down is given and the crew quietly return to their duties, enabling the ship to return to its normal patrol course.

During the rest of the day, the patrol encounters several minesweepers using their trawls to free mines anchored to the seabed, triggering feelings in Robert that cause him to question his choice of role in the RNPS. He could have remained a trawlerman to feed the country or he could have joined the minesweepers doing their critical role. Having spoken to the men of the minesweeper crews back at the Nest, he respects them greatly. They do a vital job and use techniques that have been learned and practised by trawlerman for many years. The intricacies of the trawl equipment and the coordination between the sweeping ships fascinate him, and while this seems better than just steaming up and down a patrol sector, he worries about their vulnerability. There is always the danger from a swept mine hitting the ship, but the greater concern is the vulnerability they face when they are unable to manoeuvre themselves to defend against attack.

Reflecting on his choice to be on patrol vessels, he concludes he is better off, as it must be safer to fight back.

On Friday the crew are relieved to be finishing their patrol as they start the journey back to Harwich and the relative safety of port. They all want to freshen up and run ashore to enjoy the pubs, or maybe a local show, anything to take their minds away from their first experience of the enemy and their shocking involvement with the mine. Robert has worked out the port watches based on a discussion with the Skipper and the whole crew are to be on board until 1800 hours, carrying out maintenance, replenishment of stores and general cleaning activities. Shore leave is granted to those who are not covering the watch between 1800 and 0000 hours. Each harbour watch requires two people who can cover each so a simple pattern is produced. The Skipper and Bowes take the first watch from 2000 to 0000, while Robert puts himself on the middle watch with Thomas, leaving Locke and Hall to pick up the morning watch.

As Robert is not on duty until 0000 he takes the chance to write to his family at home but avoids any mention of the danger he has started to feel following his first patrol. Missing his family enormously he wants to tell them of his feelings, but he knows he is not a great letter writer, and he could easily say the wrong thing. Previously, when he left on a fishing trip for up to a week there was no opportunity to write and therefore he has had very little practise at putting his thoughts and feelings on paper. Remoteness is a challenge for him, as there is little he can do as was shown during the recent oil fire danger. Protecting his family is his responsibility, yet he has chosen to be on the other side of the country, protecting all the country's families. It is not lost on him that this is true for so many men in similar situations and had they not chosen to answer the call to defend the country, everyone would suffer. Missing his family is the cost of serving this higher cause.

He finishes his letter and takes a stroll to free his mind from the thoughts that cloud it. A post box at the end of the street is conveniently located to send his letter home. As he walks slowly, he takes in the noise and merriment from a nearby pub, wondering if any of his crew are inside, joining the locals to share an end of the week drink. It would be easy to go inside and join them for a quick drink, but he is currently comfortable with his own company and he needs to head back to the ship for his watch. He is not expecting to get any sleep until 0400 and only time will tell if it is the deep sleep of a man at ease with his situation, or if his worries re-emerge to be amplified by the solitude of his bunk.

Chapter 8

The Rescue

6th September 1940 - Harwich

Approaching midnight, the men return from the pub. George Thomas finds Robert in the aft cabin and hands him a copy of a newspaper. Pointing at a small headline, George holds the paper and Robert takes it with his eyes fixed on a story detailing how the Pembroke Dock oil fire has finally been extinguished.

'Thank you, George. The fire is finally over. It says here that it took eighteen days to put out. That's great news.'

'Glad to hear it, Robert. I saw the paper in the Pub and knew you were still worried about the ongoing fire at home.' George has a big family and has always shown his support and care for Robert as their situations are so alike. Looking at Robert he sees a man who has just had the weight of the world lifted from his shoulders.

Robert smiles and gets ready for his watch.

Earlier that day the Caithness was stocked up with fuel and loaded with new provisions. Now at midnight, the ship welcomes the crew following their refreshing run ashore. Robert and Thomas prepare for the middle watch by checking over the engine room and the rest of the ship before they settle down in the wheelhouse where there are collapsible chairs, and they can take an opportunity to talk over the last few days on patrol.

'Do you think that destroyer we saw on Monday was laying mines,' asks Thomas.

'I don't think it was. I think it was travelling too fast when we saw it, but it could easily have been laying them earlier in the evening. It is a terrible business and there are reports of many being killed by enemy mines as the days go by. It just shows how close the enemy is getting to us.'

After a long pause, Thomas adds, 'This is only the start. I think there are going to be a huge number of mines laid and we will have our work cut out trying to protect the minesweepers as they try to keep the lanes open. If it's as easy as dropping them from the back of a destroyer then what chance do we have.'

Robert is desperate to think of something positive to say but all he can add is, 'we'll have to find a way to stop them. We can't let them have a free run at us like this. They are using U-Boats as well.'

'What do you suggest.'

'Well, I don't know to be honest. I think we just need to do what is asked of us and do it well. I don't mean just blindly follow orders and leave it to others. I think we need to remember how well we know the sea and use that to our advantage.'

'How?' enquires Thomas.

'Well, we can start by seeing more than we are. We have a lookout on each watch, with the leader and the helmsman scanning the sea, but we need to see the threats early. We need to treat all movement on the water as the enemy. Seeing is not enough, we need to observe the detail, and that's where we can make a difference. We can't just say we've seen an enemy aeroplane or a ship passing us, we need to say exactly what is happening and identify enemy craft, give good descriptions, be precise with headings and say what course we think they're on,' adds Robert.

He sees Thomas' head nodding, but he is not offering any more to the discussion. Surprised at his own clarity of thought in this area, he considers how he has done this in the past on fishing trips and how it has kept him safe. Just seeing bad weather approaching, or tides changing, won't keep you safe, you need to learn how to observe these things and take meaning from them.

They start talking about more general things and eventually they get around to some gossip about others in the crew. Robert is restless given the seriousness of the previous conversation and feels he should find a completely new way to spend the time.

'Can you take me down to the engine room as I'm keen to know more about this ship and how it works?'

'Yes, I should check out things anyway, so let's pay a visit.'

Thomas leads the way as Robert follows him down the steps, across the main deck and through the galley to the mess room ladder that descends into the Engine room.

'Sorry about that,' apologies Robert. 'I'm making all these comments about seeing and observing things and you're stuck down here without any view of what's happening on the decks above.'

'Well, I know you're right because we've only done one patrol in her but I'm trying to learn more about what this ship is telling me. I'm listening out for noises and rhythms that can tell me things that I won't get from just the dials. These extra details seem the same as the observations you are referring to.'

'Thanks for that, I do know what you mean. I'm just not sure how to explain this to the men or the Skipper.'

'Well, something will come to you.'

There is a pause while both men consider the lengths they are going to so they can remain one step ahead.

'Now, I know a bit about these steam engines, but this one is bigger than the one I'm used to on my trawler.'

'You probably have seen smaller compound steam engines, but this is a triple expansion engine and has an extra stage. Here, let me show you. Do you have time?', asks Thomas as he moves further into the engine room.

'Yes, I'm keen to see.'

Thomas grabs a torch and starts shining it on some overhead pipework, through the simple two furnace Scotch boiler and onto the triple-expansion steam engine beyond.

'What is the weak point down here?'

'That's the boiler. You must treat it very carefully as it does not behave well if you fire it badly. You need to bring it up to temperature slowly, so the expansion is evenly spread. When you get it wrong you'll get leaks in the pipes passing through the boiler and then you've got a big job to fix it. You can't learn this stuff in a book. You need to make mistakes and get bitten before you know your way around down here. I'll keep you moving, Robert, just keep us safe up there.'

'I'll do my bit.'

The harbour layover boosts the crew even though it was just for one night. Saturday morning has arrived, and the Caithness leaves its dockside berth for its second patrol. There is a relatively calm sea on this beautiful summer morning and the slight sea state is a godsend to those on board who are nursing themselves into the day, following the previous night's drinking. Robert missed out on the shore-based revelry, but he was glad of the good news from home and the small chance of some rest. He oversaw maintenance during the day ashore and felt he had made a good effort with the task of writing home. No letters have arrived for Harwich ships, so the men are missing out on much-needed family contact.

Good visibility from the wheelhouse on this clear morning helps Robert lead the forenoon watch as the ship heads out to sea. Bound once more for their patrol sector just north of the Aldeburgh Light Ship, their orders are to keep watch over minesweepers and report on any unusual activity in the area. News and updates from HQ focus on the increase in enemy minelaying efforts along the whole east coast, with some as far south as the Thames Estuary. The enemy's overall strategy is to stop shipping from reaching the Port of London, but mines are a danger anywhere the convoys pass along the complete length of the protective corridor. Naturally, this is of great concern to the Royal Navy commanders and their orders reflect the imperatives designed to protect the vital convoy routes, irrespective of the limited available resources.

Leading the patrol, the Caithness is travelling at the head of a convoy of four converted trawlers, configured differently from the first patrol, as two ships were given different orders this time out. The shore base commander, F.O.I.C. Harwich, instructs them to improve on the details contained in the signals they send and to increase the speed of responses to the telegraph communications from HQ. Discussing the details in their orders, the Skipper and Robert both agree to work hard to overcome the concerns that have been raised. Both senior men agree that their telegraph operators are both well trained, so the problem is not with the transmission, but clearly with the content and how soon signals get to the watch leader. Robert is keen to talk to the telegraphists and work through some ideas to help improve the flow of information.

Eight bells sound and the forenoon watch ends with Robert catching the telegraph operators' attention as they change over.

'Locke, can you stay for five minutes?'

'Yes.'

Robert explains the situation, 'We have a couple of problems with the signals we are sending. HQ want more details so the Skipper and me need to give you more details to send. That's an easy one to fix.'

Both Lock and Bowes nod their agreement at this obvious statement.

'Now the other problem is how quickly we reply to any questions HQ is asking us. If you receive a signal you cannot leave the wireless room to get the attention of the watch leader, or you may miss another signal and that's not good, especially at the height of action stations. What can we arrange here to improve things?'

Bowes offers up a suggestion. 'I think we need to rig up a pully and thin rope to allow travel across the wheelhouse roof, so the wireless operator can sound the ship's bell when there is a message. What do you think?'

'That can work,' responds Robert.

'Yes,' offers Bowes, 'we'd need to keep it to a special ring combination, so it does not get confused with other bell sounds.'

'Right, that can work. It's just that the wheelhouse was not designed to work as a fighting ship. We have to think up some ways around these challenges,' suggests Robert. 'Let's see if it works on the next watch. Over to you Bowes. Get some help from the engine room boys if you need to drill holes or other fixings.'

'Right, let me get to work.'

Robert explains the plan they have to the Skipper and he seems happy to give this new approach a try. A purpose-built navy ship would have a better design around the operation of the ship when it is on patrol or at action stations. Modern warships have a communication system that allows key crew members to communicate with the watch leader and Skipper, using headsets and cables. A trawler has no need for closed communication systems and as a result, they have to create their own ways to operate the ship and keep HQ informed.

This patrol's first day and night are incident free, but there is a general shift in the signal traffic as reports build a picture of the enemy's switch to bombing London. So many families now come into the direct line of the bomb aimer's sights. Everyone agrees this is a significant change in the war's direction and a clear prelude to any invasion.

The watches are working well on Sunday, with a good sense of the crew getting to know each other, as stories of the night ashore are uncovered, and the exploits of the younger men are a target for ribbing from the older trawlermen.

Robert leads the morning watch and looks forward to it ending at 0800 so he can get his breakfast. The lookout knocks on the wheelhouse window and calls Robert out to the bridge. The lookout points skyward at two aircraft heading south in the opposite direction to their course through the water. The men have been trained on plane spotting, and the enemy aeroplanes are not difficult to identify as their distinctive shape is usually all that is needed. Recognised as a Dornier, it raises concern as it is a type of bomber often used to target patrol ships and minesweepers.

Robert is slow to react as he follows the aeroplanes, but he recovers and reaches for the ship's bell and calls the crew to action stations. Quickly men are manning the main gun, the starboard Lewis gun, and soon Slater moves from lookout to use the port side Lewis gun. Adjusting the machine gun mounts so they can be aimed skywards, both guns take aim and Robert moves around the bridge to help with the spotting. The Skipper is in the wheelhouse and Robert opens the door to speak to him.

'Can we open fire Skipper?'

'Yes, if you are sure it's the enemy.'

'We're sure,' replies Robert and returning to Slater he gives the order to open fire. The two men watch as the machine gun tracer shells head into the sky.

'They are too far away,' announces the Skipper who has joined them outside. 'What are they?'

'Dornier light bombers Sir,' answers Slater without thinking.

'Yes, they are close to a mile away and at that height we can't touch them. Ceasefire,' orders Robert and tracks the aeroplanes as they continue south. Adding, 'We must call this into Harwich as a priority,' as he heads to the wheelhouse to speak to Locke in the wireless room.

'Make sure you emphasise that this could be an attack on patrol vessels, Crawford,' shouts the Skipper to ensure Robert hears him.

Returning, Robert asks, 'All the details have been sent to Harwich. Are we good to stand down?'

'Yes. Carry on,' declares the Skipper with an air of annoyance that shows he is not happy with their effectiveness against the aeroplanes.

'Stand down,' orders Robert as the gun crews return to their duties.

Robert joins Slater at the front of the bridge, and they continue scanning the sky.

'What do you make of that Slater?'

'Well, it will be tough to do anything against aeroplanes at that distance. They weren't trying to attack us so where were they heading?'

'I don't know, but this is something new for us to look out for. I think we need to report all sightings to see if anyone at Harwich can work out what's happening.'

Soon, the watch completes, and breakfast is calling. The mess room is full of talk about the aeroplanes and there is a lot of speculation on the enemy's intended purpose. Many theories are offered. The talking and speculation continue as the forenoon watch starts, and Robert heads for some well-earned rest.

Later that afternoon Robert is in the wheelhouse and Locke calls him into the wireless room to hand him a recently arrived signal. The two men stare at each other after the message is read and Robert decides to ask Slater to lead the watch while he visits the Skipper in the wardroom.

The Skipper invites him in asking, 'what's the problem?'

'It's a message from Harwich, sir,' explains Robert, 'The bombers we saw this morning attacked minesweepers operating in Gap E. One minesweeper has been sunk and another has picked up survivors. We have been ordered to rendezvous with the minesweeper and transfer the survivors over to a destroyer. This will let the minesweeper return to sweeping the gap.'

'That is bad news. Make plans for the rendezvous and let the crew know what is happening.'

'Yes sir. I'll speak to the men to make sure the lookouts know what to look for as we head for the minesweeper's location. I'll also let them know about the transfer to the destroyer. This will be a shock, but it will remind the men that we have an important job to do here.'

Both men part in silence.

After a short trip around the ship to informing the crew of their orders, Robert is back in the wheelhouse to continue the afternoon watch. Having turned the ship, they are travelling south towards Gap E, when suddenly, he lowers his binoculars and moves to call action stations via the ships bell.

The Skipper enters the wheelhouse.

'What's happening, Crawford?'

'There's a fast-moving craft about to pass across our bow, some twelve hundred yards ahead. Do you see it, sir?'

'Let me see. Where are my binoculars? Have any enemy sightings come over in the signals?'

'No, sir. I've asked Bowes to signal the rest of the patrol to see if they have seen anything, but the replies so far say nothing.'

'Very good Crawford.'

'Sir, I've been focusing on the wake from the craft. Do you think it's an E-Boat? We've not seen one yet but it's small and very fast.'

'Yes, it looks like the type of craft we've been warned about. Do you think we can hit it?'

'No sir, not at this distance or at the speed it is moving. The gun crew need to stay alert in case it changes course and comes too close.'

Both men search for any sign of an alteration in the mystery craft's path.

'Half ahead' shouts the Skipper as he uses the engine room telegraph to change speed, and the scanning of the sea continues. The craft crosses the trawler's path and continues towards the coast at high speed.

'So that must have been an E-Boat sir, with the speed it was moving at. That was fast! We should signal that into F.O.I.C. Harwich, giving as much detail on speed and direction as we can. We also need to tell the other patrol vessels of these details so they can keep an eye out for it returning.'

'Yes, Crawford. We can stand down all hands and go back to the watches.'

The Skipper shouts, 'stand down all hands, full ahead,' as the engine room telegraph signals the speed change, and the command is acknowledged from below.

'Aye, sir,' replies Robert as he leaves the wheelhouse and calls to the men to stand down from the 12-Pounder and the Lewis guns.

Before leaving, the Skipper and Robert discuss the recent sighting and they both agree that their first encounter with an enemy E-Boat was fast and fleeting. While discussing the threat, the Skipper provides some details that have been given to him as part of a general briefing by the Royal Navy. The E-Boat name comes from the British designation for Enemy, but the original name is Schnellboot, meaning "fast boat". These attack craft run out of occupied ports in France and the low countries. With a top speed of over forty knots, the E-Boats aim to attack any ships involved in the protection of the North Sea and if they take control they will wreak havoc on British shipping convoys and jeopardise the whole operation to supply the country. Robert believes they reacted quickly to the first sighting of the craft and they have helped by giving as much detail as possible to the patrol and to Harwich. Thinking ahead Robert considers what they must do if they have a similar encounter, at closer range, or with better visibility. They must have options and a plan to attack the next E-Boat they encounter.

Continuing the afternoon watch, they turn east as they pass Aldeburgh lightship, and enter Gap E, slowing to half ahead as they near the rendezvous point. Slater is quick to identify a ship travelling southwest and roughly heading for the same position as them. Slater calls Robert to the bridge, via a tap on the wheelhouse window and the two men meet to scrutinise the approaching ship through their binoculars, quickly reaching the view that they are looking at a British trawler. The shape of the vessel is a clear indicator of its type and there is also the hint of a white ensign flying from the rear mast.

'Looks like the minesweeper we're looking for Second-Hand. What's its name?

'Yes, we're looking for HMT Malvern. I must get Locke to radio this in.'

'Can we signal the ship approaching us from the northeast?'

'Not easily without a call sign. We should attempt to contact her with the signal lamp as that will be quicker. Bowes is your best bet to do that,' suggests Locke. Robert heads off to find Bowes and eventually locates him in the mess room enjoying some sandwiches and a cup of tea. They both head back to the wheelhouse and the signal lamp is readied for use.

'What shall I signal?' asks Bowes.

'Approaching ship, identify yourself, and state your destination,' instructs Robert, as Bowes operates the signal lamp from the bridge. They wait for a reply and none is seen.

'Try again Bowes,' asks Robert and the command is carried out. After a short while, there is a flashing light visible via their binoculars and Bowes reads out each word as it arrives.

'Patrol ship … HMT Malvern … carrying … casualties … from … minesweeper … attacked … off … Gap E.'

'Right, signal back telling them who we are and that we'll wait to transfer their casualties,' orders Robert. Bowes starts to hit the shutter leaver to send the Morse code signal flashes towards the approaching ship.

'They are acknowledging, Second-Hand. HMT Caithness … thank … you … for … your … offer … we … have ….'

The message halts as a huge explosion erupts in the eyepieces of the Caithness men. Lowering their binoculars, they take in the full horror of the view ahead and are struck speechless as a plume of water shoots high into the air as the distant ship is overwhelmed by flame and smoke. The Malvern has been lifted into the air and then buckled and folded at its middle as it drops back on the water. A second explosion follows as the bow and stern rise out of the water, gradually moving towards each other, as the sea sucks the two parts of the ship down into a maelstrom of churning water.

Reaching instinctively for the ship's bell, Robert sounds action stations. The crew respond well in the circumstances as he enters the wheelhouse to instruct the helmsman to change course, operating the engine room telegraph himself to gain speed towards the Malvern's last position.

'What's happening, Crawford?' asks the Skipper in a slightly panicked voice, as he enters the wheelhouse.

'Sir, we were signalling a ship we'd just established was HMT Malvern, when there was an almighty explosion and the ship floundered and sank very quickly. I've changed course and speed to see if there are any survivors.'

'Well done, Crawford, carry on.'

Robert re-joins Bowes and Slater on the bridge and asks, 'did you see any E-Boats or aeroplanes in the area before that explosion?'

'No.'

'Me neither.'

'So, it must be a U-Boat or a mine. We must all keep a lookout as we rush to rescue any survivors. We can't suffer the same fate as they did,' says

Robert to the men, and as much to himself, as he weighs up the risks.

He must signal Harwich to inform them of the sinking but also to see if there are any U-Boat sightings. He leaves the details of what to report, and what to ask, with Locke and returns to the wheelhouse. Pulling out a chart of the area he explains his concerns to the Skipper.

'Sir, we didn't see any aeroplanes or E-Boats while we were looking out at the Malvern. We're sure there was nothing we could see that could have attacked the ship above the sea. That leaves a U-Boat or a mine, and I've looked at these charts and I cannot see a U-Boat working in these unpredictable depths at low tide and so close to the barrier mines. There are deeper channels close by so we can't rule that out. But I'm guessing this must have been a mine dropped earlier by an enemy aircraft.'

'I agree,' is the short reply from the Skipper.

Robert does not know what to do other than say, 'Aye, sir,' as he re-joins Bowers and Slater where they are maintaining lookout. Following him, the Skipper helps with lookout duty and provides some reprieve to the men on the bridge.

'I must join the main gun crew,' says Bowes, mindful of his allocated station.

Peering down at the gun and only seeing four men, Robert agrees with Bowes. Given they are following up a sinking, they need maximum observation coverage and protection as it would be all too easy to focus on the rescue mission and be caught out by an attack on themselves.

Robert decides to speak to Fredricks and Harris who are manning the Lewis guns. Explaining his theory, Robert believes that a mine sank the Malvern, but as there is so much aircraft and E-Boat activity in general, he does not want anything getting close to them. He can trust both men to keep their eyes open to any threat.

Joining Slater, he knows that if a mine was dropped overnight by an aeroplane, then it would be sitting below the water, tethered to an anchor block. With no chance of seeing another mine as they glide through the water, he hopes the drop pattern is wide enough to allow them to get to the last position of the Malvern unharmed.

Reducing its speed to dead slow ahead, the Caithness draws close to the site of the explosion, while they all feel the strain as they measure their progress in feet and inches. Robert feels the blood pounding in his ears as he observes burning oil and debris floating on the surface. Those on the bridge hear the muted cries of men and turn their search in that direction. Slater spots the men clinging to an unrecognisable part of the ship that is keeping them afloat. Running into the wheelhouse, Robert shows Stanford where he wants him to position the ship, and he carefully guides the trawler, so its starboard side comes in close to the stricken men. Slater leaves lookout duties to the Skipper as he joins Robert as they both make their way to the side of the ship on the main deck, where they are joined by the main gun crew. Together they lift the survivors out of the water and Robert settles them down against the side of the ship to let them recover. He asks them if they have seen any other men following the explosion, but they say they have not seen or heard anyone else.

Easing the ship around the waterborne wreckage, the Caithness crew are now standing at the bow and to the sides looking directly into the sea, hoping to find more survivors. Robert says a prayer for those that have perished but his remaining hope does not last long, and they decide to return to the patrol channel and the relative safety of the swept sector. Robert plots a short course that takes them back through Gap E, using exactly the same route as they took to advance towards the wreckage. He does not want to travel through yet more unknown water and risk the possibility of discovering another mine. The Caithness performs the nautical equivalent of retracing its own footsteps.

Approaching the rescued men, Robert asks, 'so who can tell me what happened?'

One man stands slowly and says, 'I'm off the Malvern and so is Joe here,' pointing to the man closest to him. 'We'd rescued a few men from the sea earlier this afternoon after they'd hit what we thought was a mine. This chap here was one of the men we rescued,' pointing to the man furthest away from him who looked to have a badly injured leg.

'I see,' says Robert as he attempts a sympathetic tone. 'Where were you on the ship when the explosion happened?'

'Well, we had taken the rescued men aft, so they were on deck between our launch boats. We laid them down on blankets and cabin seat cushions, where someone who knew what to do was bandaging them up. Then the explosion happened.'

'Were you thrown clear?'

'Well, I can't remember. The next thing I know is I'm in the water and I see these other two here. One of the launch boats was overturned next to me so I pulled the others over so we could grip the rear where the rudder was.'

'Did you hear anyone else in the water?'

'No. I kept shouting out but there was no answer. A lot of the men we'd rescued were in a bad way so they probably could not save themselves in the water. There were only two other Malvern crew on deck, and I didn't see them again.'

Reaching out to hold the man's arm, Robert says, 'Look you're shaking. Let's get you warm and comfortable and I'll make arrangements to transfer you to a larger ship to get you heading back to Harwich. They'll be able to check you over in their sickbay and get you ashore.'

'Thank you,' says the shivering man. 'You saved our lives!'

'You'd have done the same for us. Now let us take care of you,' adds Robert as he leads the man to the warmth of the galley, as four crewmen step forward to help with the other two survivors.

Robert finds their story of escape fascinating and almost unbelievable, especially for the man who has now been rescued from the sea twice in one day. He could not begin to think of the odds of that happening as he leaves the men in the care of others and makes his plans for their transfer to a ship that would return them to Harwich and to safety.

Various signals are sent back and forth to organise the transfer and eventually a plan is agreed for the Caithness to wait for a destroyer with the transfer made via small boats. The tiredness and injuries to the survivors require a boatswain's chair to be rigged to hoist them onto the larger ship. The transfer is successful, and Robert is relieved. He is sure they are simply glad to be alive.

Robert thinks back on the day as he starts the Second Dog watch. Feeling glad to have helped with the men's rescue he knows the crew upheld the best traditions of all seafarers. Today he experienced true peril and now understands for the first time that there are dangers all around. The enemy can assault them from the air in the form of aeroplanes and dropped mines, there is assault from under the sea in the shape of U-Boats and mines, and on the surface from E-Boats and destroyers. His ideas on observation and lookout practice, still need improvement. He worries how this will affect the men as they have now seen danger, and they have not been able to respond or use their weapons on something, anything. There is a very real need to feel that you are responding to an attack and not just let it happen to you. Today did not allow for a positive response, and Robert knows he will have to be quick to act in the coming days if there is going to be any chance for the crew to respond. Time will tell.

Chapter 9

Peril

9th September 1940, North Sea

It is past midnight and the early hours of Monday morning start with a calm sea and a clear moonlit sky. Patrolling is difficult in these conditions. The Caithness crew are running their watches as normal with the lookouts focusing intently on any activity on the water, especially following the previous day's experience with the lightning quick E-Boats. Earlier, while there was still light, the lookouts were also scanning the skies for any Luftwaffe activity, as dropped mines are a new additional worry following their experience with the sinking of the minesweeper.

Royal Air Force fighters were patrolling the area at the same time and the lookouts needed to accurately recognise these friendly aeroplanes and quickly distinguish them from the enemy. Levels of alertness amongst the crew are very high and this is putting everyone under strain. No one wants to let anyone else down in this situation and pressure builds as danger levels grow across this small stretch of water.

At the start of the morning watch, the Skipper is leading from the wheelhouse and he strains his eyes to see navigation lights through his binoculars. The waning moon does little to help his vision. As they travel north, he catches sight of a dark shape moving fast, approaching from the northeast. Instructing the lookout to sound the call for action stations, the Skipper continues to track the approaching craft, when Robert enters the wheelhouse asking, 'what have we got?'

'Same as the other day. Now they plan to attack under darkness. No sound. Luckily I spotted it.'

'Aye, sir,' acknowledges Robert, as he watches the crew take up their stations. He wants to see how the men respond now that he is observing a different team from his own.

Bowes pulls the cord to sound the ship's bell from the wireless room and when Robert responds he says, 'I've just checked with F.O.I.C. Harwich and it's not one of our ships, sir.'

Bringing his binoculars to the same bearing as the Skipper, Robert adds, 'looks to be on a course heading to intercept us. The crew on the main gun might not have a clear sight because of the foremast and rigging. I'll check. Can we open fire, sir?'

'Yes,' replies the Skipper as Robert heads out onto the bridge.

'Have you got a clean shot?' shouts Robert to the gun crew.

'Aye,' shouts James the leading gunlayer.

'Fire when ready,' Robert orders, and almost immediately there is a shell hurtling its way towards the dark shape closing on their position.

Immediately, Robert orders Stanford on the starboard Lewis gun to open fire and tracer rounds light up the path across the water to the approaching ship. Robert moves around the wheelhouse to the port Lewis gunners and asks Harris to keep a watch out for anything coming at them from this angle. With the starboard Lewis gun still firing, Stanford shouts, 'Reload,' and Robert hurries around to help him fit another drum holding ninety-seven rounds of ammunition. The machine gun has an effective range of over eight hundred yards and while the E-Boat is within this range, it takes hits to its superstructure.

The E-Boat's machine guns are firing at the Caithness and for some, this is the first time they have come directly under fire in any form. It leaves them terrified.

Altering course, the E-Boat travels on a parallel course to the Caithness before turning again to start on an intercept heading. This time the angle of attack is shorter. As the enemy craft turns towards the trawler the gun crew fires another shell and it misses its target by being ten feet too high. Straightaway, the gun crew realise that they are travelling over slight waves which have enough height to make aiming the gun a challenge. At this speed, the E-Boat is closing at over twenty yards a second and the urgency of the crew grows as they respond well, given their lack of experience. Reloading quickly, the crew get another shell away as the enemy closes to a distance of less than four hundred yards. Hitting the water in front of the E-Boat, the shell creates a plume of water and causes the craft to veer to port, just as a torpedo is sent into the water. The timing is split second, and the evasive course correction is not enough to change the trajectory of the torpedo that is now in the water.

Turning hard to port, the E-Boat follows a course that moves it away from the trawler and more towards the coast behind them. Briefly, this opens up the side of the fast-moving craft to the firepower of the main 12-Pounder, and the starboard Lewis gun. The shells from the main gun do not find their target but the machine gun fire is strafing the side of the E-Boat and making its mark. The gun crew are working more efficiently with each shell they fire, and the repeat fire rate is increasing to close to six rounds a minute. Robert is very pleased with the improvements they are making as the chances of hitting the target increase vastly with any improvement in the rate of fire.

As the shelling continues, the enemy craft moves away at speed, and the trawler crew remain unaware that there is a torpedo in the water, currently on an intercept course. Travelling through the water at ten knots the trawler is no match for the torpedo travelling at over forty knots. This mismatch ensures the torpedo will hit the trawler before it has travelled through the water for a distance equivalent to two lengths of its own keel. The E-Boat crew planned this and targeted the torpedo at a point half a keel length ahead of the trawler leaving it to the onboard gyroscope to keep it on course. The

Kriegsmarine use a torpedo that detonates on impact, but it also has a proximity mechanism based on the magnetic field changes created by a large metal target. The trigger mechanism in the torpedo has an arming distance that the crew will have set based on their launch distance.

As the Caithness crew watch the E-Boat disappear into the night there is a massive explosion just fifty yards off the starboard side. Rocked by the pressure wave from the underwater explosion, the trawler continues on its path, as the crew remain rooted to the spot, trying to take in what has just happened. No one yet knows that it is a prematurely detonating torpedo and there is a genuine fear, as the men remain at their posts, scanning the sea for more signs of an attack. Robert checks with the crew manning the guns and then climbs down from the wheelhouse to inspect the ship for damage, first looking over the railings as he moves up and down the port side. He cannot see any obvious damage.

Making his way down to the engine room he enquires after the men working deep in the hull, as they must be shaken, physically and mentally. The stokers and enginemen report that they heard the explosion and felt the shock wave as it hit the hull, causing one of them to be knocked off their feet. After checking on the men, Robert is keen to get a report of the state of the boilers and the engine and Thomas reports that all the machinery is working well, and they have managed to maintain their speed during this whole action. Thanking them all, Robert asks that they stay at actions stations until the Skipper gives the order to stand down.

Returning to the wheelhouse Robert asks the Skipper, 'what do you think that was, sir?'

'Most likely a torpedo from that E-Boat,' speculates the navy reserve man. 'I don't think we hit a mine as we wouldn't be here talking about it. I know the enemy are now dropping mines that are activated by the magnetic field of a ship, but the detonation was a way off the hull.'

'I think you're right. Do you want to stand the men down, sir?'

'No, I think we should stay alert for a while and see if the attacker returns. Keep the men at action stations for the remainder of this watch and then post extra lookouts through the night, Crawford. Oh, and ask Bowes to update the rest of the patrol and Harwich on what has happened.'

'Aye, sir,' replies Robert as he works out that he must do a double watch to be the extra lookout for the Skipper's current duty and then his own.

Robert approaches Harris asking, 'can you cover the rest of the middle and then do the morning watch as an extra lookout?'

'Yes, I can manage that. I'm not going to be able to sleep tonight after what's just happened.'

Robert is grateful and returns to the bridge to scan the sea for any activity. The crew are told to stand down as eight bells sounds at the end of the middle watch. Those crew coming off watch make for their cabins to rest, but many cannot sleep and sit in the messroom talking over a hot drink. The Skipper uses the time to signal Harwich, providing details of the raid, linking it to the previous night's activities, and hopefully building a picture of what the enemy is doing. The commanders at HMS Badger respond by telling the Skipper that they are seeing this as an escalation of activity in the area and they are warning all ships to be alert to E-Boat attacks.

Starting the forenoon watch, Robert thinks back to the times he has worked through the night while trawling and how often he has greeted the dawn. He carries out another inspection of the ship once the sun has risen sufficiently, and he is able to see along the length of the hull. He notices the plates are buckled along the section of the hull that is adjacent to the fish room, but the plates are not separating and there is no sign of any other damage.

Monday morning continues with clear skies and a calm sea. Breakfast is available in the galley for men coming off the morning watch, and they can tuck into eggs, bacon, and anything else the cooks have found in the storeroom. At the start of another day the men are acting with a touch of uneasiness. They are not looking forward to what the day brings let alone the thought of darkness falling and the probable return of the enemy's menacing fast boats.

The forenoon watch passes uneventfully, however, signals start to arrive indicating that enemy bombers are increasing their attacks on ships in the channel. The light bombers have switched their attacks from airfields and are spreading out to bomb Royal Navy destroyers and minesweepers.

That afternoon, Robert leads the first dog watch, with Stanford manning the helm and Slater as lookout on the bridge. Conversations in the wheelhouse are light-hearted and Stanford is carefully complaining about the different quality of food that is being served up based on whether James or Brown are in the galley. Feeding the men is always a challenge on any ship, so Robert makes a mental note to speak to James, the more skilled cook, to see if he can help Brown improve. Robert steps out onto the bridge to talk to Slater and get his opinion on the food, but Slater does not respond and is transfixed by something he can see in his binoculars.

'What is it, Slater?'

'There's a plane off the bow heading towards us, but I can't make out what it is.'

Lifting his binoculars to home in on the aeroplane Robert takes a short while to pick up the small shape in the sky. 'I can't make out what it is yet, but we're travelling southeast, and it is coming in from the southeast so it's best to assume it's an enemy plane. Probably a Heinkel bomber. Sound actions stations.'

'Action stations,' shouts Slater as he rings the ship's bell.'

Robert notes how quickly the crew respond on this occasion and he judges it to be their best time yet. The Skipper joins them on the bridge and simply says, 'where?'

'There sir, a bomber approaching us, directly above the bow. I'd say two miles out. An excellent spot by Slater.'

'I've got it. What do we think it is?'

'It's a Heinkel HE 111,' asserts Robert as he does not want any doubt in the Skipper's mind, and he believes it is a reasonable bet given the vast numbers of that type of bomber in operation.

'Good, it looks to be heading straight for us and at quite a low level. Are we its target?'

'Possibly sir,' offers Robert. 'A destroyer is a half-mile astern of us. It passed us a short while ago.'

Slater adds, 'I think it's after both ships as it's coming in too low to be missing us out.'

'Yes, you could be right. It wouldn't take much to hit us and then realign on the destroyer.'

'That's what we were thinking. They'll soon be in range, sir. Can we open fire?'

'Yes, open fire when in range.'

'Aye, sir,' says Robert in a normal voice before shouting the order, 'open fire on the approaching bomber when it's in range.'

'Aye,' comes the simple response from the main gun as Robert checks the view from the starboard Lewis gun. 'Have you got a shot there Fredricks?'

'No, the bomber is coming right in over the bow and the forward mast is in the way.'

Robert quickly opens the wheelhouse door and tells Stanford at the helm, 'port standard rudder.'

'That'll bring the ship to port, opening up a line of sight for you Fredricks.'

'Aye.'

Moving to the front of the bridge, Robert shouts to the main gun, 'We'll keep turning to port to give both Lewis guns a shot, but we'll also reduce the target for the bomber. Track him and open fire when you're ready.'

When Robert thinks the ship is close to forty-five degrees to the course of the bomber he comes to the port side of the bridge and opens the wheelhouse door that side, saying, 'rudder amidships, and keep her on that course until the bomber passes over us. Then I want you to steer hard to port until we are facing towards the rear of the bomber. Have you got that Stanford?'

'Aye.'

Turning to Harris on the port Lewis gun, Robert adds, 'you might get a crack at the Heinkel when she flies overhead. Keep a lookout at other times and let me know if you see anything.'

'Aye.'

Lewis gun ammunition is used at a fast rate, so the gunners are sparing with their bursts of fire until the range is established. Gunners on the 12-Pounder take a ranging shoot at the Heinkel and realise how hard it is to target aeroplanes even when they are flying low on a bombing run. It is now clear that the bomber is lining up on the trawler as part of its run and the crew are unloading more shells and firing more .303 rounds as the distance closes.

Starting to return fire from the machine guns mounted in its nose dome, the bullets from the bomber strafe the open decks and cause those manning the guns and wheelhouse to take cover. For the second time that day, the men come under fire and the terror is not lessened but the guns are manned and back in action quickly. The Heinkel is closing, and the range is good for the guns. The sea state is close to moderate and the gun aimers have a hard job adjusting to the ship's movement underneath them. The saving grace is the low height maintained by the Heinkel as it starts to completely fill the view of the gunner's sights.

The distance closes and there are successful hits from the Lewis guns, but nothing to take out the crew or any vital part of the aeroplane. The twin engines of the Heinkel create a fierce noise, growing as it closes on the trawler, also amplified by its lack of altitude and closeness to the sea. The intense drone of the engines is combining with the clatter of the enemy machine guns to create a chilling accompaniment to the scene. The crew on the main gun are loading and firing furiously, unleashing a shell close to once every ten seconds. Those watching on the bridge are willing the guns to hit their target and end this horrifying contact with the enemy. Robert feels his heart pounding in his chest, and although he lowered his binoculars a while ago to better judge the distance to the bomber, his grip on them is so tight his knuckles are white. The enemy crew are now discernible in the cockpit and abruptly it is not just machine against machine, but men against men.

Finally, a shell from the trawler's main gun hits the Heinkel, but there is no explosion. It is not obvious what damage has been done, but the bomber is clearly moving off its current course. The Caithness crew are unaware of the damage to the control wires running through the fuselage, as the bomber continues to fly, fully powered by its two engines. Struggling to maintain control of his aircraft the pilot fights with his control as the bomber loses height and slows. Crossing the line of the bow, it starts to appear on the port side of the trawler, flying increasingly closer to the sea. There is no height for the crew to bail out and the skill of the pilot is tested to the extreme as the nose dips lower and lower before eventually touching the waves. The starboard wing digs into the water first and causes the bomber to rotate violently and skim over the sea without breaking up. The bomber pauses on the surface while the occupants discover it is taking on water and they start evacuating the fuselage. The enemy crewmen are all out of the Heinkel and inflating their buoyance aids when the aeroplane starts to sink below the sea.

The Skipper telegraphs to the engine room to slow to one-third ahead and orders the helmsman to come up alongside the men in the water, keeping them on the port side. Robert is ordered to get the Leigh-Enfield rifles from their store and post crew members from the forward gun along the deck. Covering the men in the sea, they ensure no one is armed and able to fire on the ship. The trawler comes close to the aircrew in the water and ropes are lowered over the port side, allowing the men to scramble over the side of the hull and appear on the deck in a sodden state. With rifles pointed at them, the aircrew raise their hands and start to spread out along the edge of the deck, looking at the trawler crew with expressions of relief mixed with bewilderment.

Identifying the pilot by his uniform, the Skipper approaches him and asks, 'do any of you speak English?'

The pilot officer replies, 'yes I do, I am Oberleutnant Fischer, hello!' as he stands to attention and salutes to the Skipper.

'Hello, I am Lieutenant Robinson, Royal Naval Reserve. Welcome aboard.'

After a pause, the Skipper turns and orders, 'Crawford check these airmen for any weapons and then get them to sit on the deck. Use Oberleutnant Fischer to tell them not to move and keep them covered with the rifles while I signal Harwich and get some instructions on what to do with our new passengers.'

'Aye, sir.' Replies Robert. 'Alright, Brown and Altman, check them for weapons and then get them to sit down.'

The two men check the prisoners one by one for hidden weapons, and as they work down the line of the five aircrew there is a shove and Brown is pushed to the deck. The airman doing the pushing pulls a knife from the rear of his belt and lunges at Altman.

There is a shot fired and the knife-wielding prisoner crumples to the deck. James is standing holding his raised rifle, with a small trickle of smoke rising from the barrel, as the rest of the crew and prisoners are frozen to the spot. The Skipper stands on the bridge and shouts down to the crew.

'What just happened?'

'One of the prisoners attacked Brown with a knife and James has opened fire and killed him, I think,' replies Robert.

'Make sure they are unarmed and guard them closely,' barks the Skipper, as he returns inside the wheelhouse to continue with signals to F.O.I.C. Harwich.

Robert gets the crew to finish the checks on the prisoners and ensures they are sitting on the deck and unable to lunge and attack the men pointing rifles at them. This situation does not change for a good while until Robert meets the Skipper at the base of the wheelhouse ladder. The Skipper reveals that they have orders to return to their course and continue their patrol until they can rendezvous with a destroyer making its way to their location. They are to transfer the prisoners to the destroyer and the dead airman is to be returned to the sea.

The crew are tense, and some are shocked by seeing the airman killed before their eyes. James does not seem phased by the shooting and there is a steely coldness to his role guarding the men. Robert sees the contrast to how James serves the men from the galley, with his hospitality making a big difference to the collective mood of the ship, and he wonders how this difference came about. He makes a mental note to have a chat with James when this situation is over so he can try to understand what is happening.

Robert arranges for the dead airman to be placed over the side in as dignified a way as he can manage. The pool of blood on the deck is washed away and there is an attempt to scrub the stain from the oak planking, but it will persist there for some time yet.

It is now 1900 hours and Robert is called to the wheelhouse.

'Yes, sir.'

'Thank you, Crawford. We've received a signal telling us to meet a destroyer at 0015 hours just off the Aldeburgh lightship. Please ensure we are at the rendezvous point at the end of the first watch.'

'Yes, sir.'

'I'd like us to come to action stations at that point as we'll be stopped to transfer the men under darkness. There are bound to be E-Boats in the area, and we are going to be vulnerable to attack.'

'Understood, sir,' answers Robert before leaving the wheelhouse to explain the plan to the crew ahead of the start of the next watch.

HMS Govan, a destroyer, is with them at 0020 hours as they wait at the Aldeburgh lightship. One of the sixteen-foot boats from the trawler is launched over the side to make the journey to the larger ship. Lowering the prisoners into the boat they are joined by four crew who crowd in with two to row and two to cover the men with rifles. The Lewis gun also covers the boat, but only if any of the aircrew jump into the sea, as any firing from the gunner would be sure to take out the crew as well. The boat comes alongside the destroyer and a cargo net is used to bring the airmen aboard. The deck of the large ship is empty apart from a detachment of Marines who cover the prisoners as they climb up the side of the hull. Despite the darkness, Robert is happy that the transfer goes well and is relieved to be passing the prisoners on to the Royal Navy for transfer back to Harwich. Getting back to the patrol and remaining alert is his priority.

HMS Govan steams off at full speed as the Caithness turns and heads off on a northerly course at a much more modest pace. The trawler is still under action stations while the destroyer is tracked from the bridge. All those present see a colossal explosion, so they turn the trawler and steam to the location of the devastation to start a search for survivors. There is no sign of the destroyer, apart from floating and burning wreckage. Signals are calling several ships into the area to carry out searches and another destroyer is soon on hand.

Robert is sickened to his core at the loss of life of the crew of such a large ship. He is physically sick at the sight of what he has just witnessed, and it takes some time to compose himself. He later learns that twenty-five crew were picked up and were the only survivors. An E-Boat was responsible and there is a fresh case of death and destruction delivered by one of these small craft.

At night the E-Boats are a constant threat, and the patrol ships are as watchful as they can be, often keeping the enemy at bay with machine gun fire and the occasional shell. After five nights the Caithness returns to Harwich. The crew welcome the sight of the harbour and are glad to be ashore for a night. Robert will never forget the loss of life he has seen on this patrol. This brutal war has changed him forever.

Chapter 10

Taking Stock

12th September 1940, Pembroke Dock

It is a week since the Luftwaffe switched its focus away from RAF targets to concentrate on bombing London and other cities. Newspapers carry details from war correspondents that outline the horror of sustained attacks on the country. Everyone is reminded that the country is still under threat of invasion.

Alice's father visits as he wants to know how well she is coping with the children on her own. She reminds him that she is used to Robert being at sea for weeklong trips and the current situation is simply an extension of that way of living.

'Alice, have you seen the newspapers today?'

'No, I haven't had time to go to the shops yet. You are quite early visiting. Is something wrong?'

'Well, there are some stark warnings about the invasion in the newspaper and I wanted to know your thoughts.'

'Father, I haven't given it much thought. There is a lot of fighting to be done before an invasion can happen.'

'I agree, but we need to plan ahead. I'd like you and the children to come and stay with us in

Pembroke, at least until we know which way the war is heading.'

'What good would that do? I intend to stay here and look after the house until Robert has time to come home on leave,' replies Alice, as she stands firm knowing her father is only doing what any father would do in the circumstances.

'Look, I'm concerned that you are not thinking this through. You cannot wait until there are Nazi soldiers marching down the street outside. People will be segregated, and atrocities will be committed. Think of the children.'

'I am thinking of the children. I want to keep them here in the house they know, and I will cope with any situations that develop. What extra protection can you provide at your house?'

'There will be more of us there and while I'm just into my sixties I can still help protect you.'

Seeing the fear and love in his eyes Alice backs down from a full-scale argument and tries to see the situation more from his perspective. Pausing, she responds, 'I understand your concern. I'll think about it and let you know at the weekend. Is that alright?'

'Yes, I'm happy if you agree to think about it. I lie awake at night thinking of how much danger you're in with the raids that have occurred on the town since the start of the month.'

Remembering the recent destruction of a house in Arthur Street, Alice is upset and knows it has been the same for all her neighbours. Fortunately, the occupants of the house escaped unharmed as they protected themselves in their garden's Anderson Shelter. Despite this close call, there is a lot of speculation, as many theories are offered for the real target of the bombs that night.

Llanion Army Barracks back onto Arthur Street and is an obvious target for the attack. Many people point to the location of the Llanion Oil Storage Depot directly behind the barracks. This oil storage depot is a mirror copy of the Llanreath depot found on the opposite side of the town. It was the Llanreath depot that was bombed in August with disastrous results, and many believe the civilian house destruction was a simple overshoot of a few hundred yards from the original target of the Llanion depot.

It is unthinkable that they came so close to another fire that would have threatened and devastated the town. Only last week, hundreds of firemen won their eighteen-day battle against the Llanreath fire by extinguishing the blaze that had consumed millions of gallons of fuel. The bombing raid on the Tremeyrick Street house was launched four days before the Llanreath fire was extinguished, and with this timing in mind, the fire services believe they would have been unable to cope with the overlapping devastation. The enemy's timing was a clear opportunity to split the fire services attention and their failure to hit the designated target is well received by the town's people. Collectively, everyone wonders what is coming next.

Alice has a few more minutes of civil conversation with her father before he makes his excuses and leaves. Reminding her that she agreed to think about his offer, he steps into his car and is soon travelling down the road. As Alice is left standing on the pavement, she looks around and can see little of any of the dangers that surrounded her. A short walk to one end of the street would bring the Llanion camp and oil tanks into view while walking the other way would bring the dockyard and the Sunderland base into her line of sight.

Climbing the steps to the house she turns towards the pleasant green expanse of the hill reaching up towards the Defensible Barracks and believes she has been guilty of dismissing the dangers that surround her and the children. Her father's offer needs serious thought. Pembroke is only two miles away, and it must be the safer option given the high-value targets close to her home.

The day continues with normal routine as the schools have started back and the two oldest children are now attending. Alice and James make the most of the day before taking the short walk to Albion Square school to fetch the others.

The evening passes pleasantly, and Alice is only briefly drawn back to the distressing memories of the day's earlier conversations. After the children are tucked up in bed she decides she must sit down and write to Robert. However, there are very conflicting words in Alice's head as she attempts to compose a letter that will boost his situation and not reflect on her recent realisations. Progress on the letter is slow and Alice retires early.

There is a strange noise in Alice's head that disturbs her from a deep sleep. Focusing on the noise, she tries to remove her confusion, but it is hard to understand the cause and it takes a while before she concludes it is real and not the product of her vivid dreams. Her heart pounds as she collects her dazed thoughts and recognises the sound. It is an air raid siren.

Rushing from under the blankets she collects her dressing gown in a single sweeping motion and has it wrapped around herself before she enters one of the children's rooms to rouse them. Swinging around the door to wake the others there is a slow reaction to her calls and she must repeat them with more urgent cries. With all three children awake and alert, she moves them downstairs in the dark. Tired and half asleep they carefully make their way towards the cellar door. Alice has fitted blackout curtains to the whole house, and this includes the cellar's window positioned below the pavement level. So with confidence, she turns on the cellar light from the top of the stairwell, and they descend in dim light, one uneven step at a time.

The children are frightened and timidly ask what is happening. Alice is very unsure what to say but tries to reassure them by telling them they have come into the cellar to be safe while there are men above fighting and making lots of loud noises.

The siren continues to wail, and the long wait begins for the all-clear to sound. A muffled explosion is heard, and Alice attempts to pinpoint the direction and distance of the sound, but she finds it impossible from down in the cellar. Shortly, there is a second explosion, and it is immediately apparent that the distance has shortened, and the deadly object has landed a lot closer to their house. The children are very distressed, tired and lack any understanding of what is happening to them. Whimpering rather than crying out, Alice hates to see their reaction as it reflects their deep terror and also chills her to the bone.

Another explosion follows, and the whole house is shaken to its foundations, causing them all to cling to one another more tightly. The cellar window clatters violently, and it is a huge relief that it does not blow inwards, catapulting shards of glass towards their cowering bodies. Realising the bomb has landed close to the house, Alice has no intention of looking through the cellar window or venturing upstairs without the children. They wait for the all-clear signal.

Unknown to Alice an upstairs window has been broken, not by the shockwave from the explosion, but by a large fragment of shrapnel that was ejected from the exploding bomb casing. Smashing through the window of the front room of the house, the fragment hits the back wall, before dropping onto the carpet. The heat from the explosion is transferred from the shrapnel to the carpet and it starts to smoulder.

Waiting in the cellar Alice listens out for another explosion and believes she hears two distant rumbles that could be part of the same attack. Listening again there is relief as the all-clear siren sounds and they can leave their dark confines. Opening the door at the top of the steps Alice has the children at her feet directly in front of her. As the door opens into the darkness there is the unmistakable smell of burning. Rapidly assessing the situation, Alice sees that there is smoke coming through the open door to the front room. This door is situated to their left at the end of the hallway, close to the front door of the house. She ushers the children through the kitchen door to their right and closes it behind them. Approaching the front room door in the semi-darkness, she stares into the darkness to assess any possible fire and notices with relief that the carpet has not yet caught light. Quickly returning to the kitchen, she grabs a saucepan sitting on the draining board and fills it with water. Closing the kitchen door behind her, Alice moves purposefully back to the front room and manages to cover the smouldering section of carpet with the full amount of water she has carried. The water does its job, stopping the carpet from catching fire and cooling down the fragment of bomb casing. Steam rises from the jagged lump of metal and Alice starts to breathe normally.

The children are shouting from the kitchen and it takes a while to calm them down. After a small drink of milk, they are persuaded back to bed and settle down to sleep after some inevitable questions that are hard to answer. Alice is ill-equipped to answer given the late hour and the stress of the past forty minutes. While she is too angry to go back to bed herself, she decides to have a cup of hot milk to calm her nerves and sits at the kitchen table pondering the difficult choices she has before her. What would Robert want?

There is no point in denying that the town is becoming a more dangerous place to stay. However, she feels a stubbornness and a resistance to the attacks that originates from a clear rage felt for an enemy that is targeting and attempting to destroy her children and her home. How dare they.

Henry arrives promptly the next morning and he cannot explain his reasons for making the journey that early in the day. He is appalled by the damage to the house and takes Alice out into the road to point to a large crater that has appeared in the grass on the hill, a few dozen yards directly opposite her front door. Earth and debris are scattered over a wide area and a few people are standing around looking into the exposed crater. Neighbours are standing out on the street and speculation is rife as they attempt to comprehend the intended target for the raid.

Henry explains his anger at the situation, and he wants Alice to pack up and come with him immediately. She explains that she will not be rushed into such a big decision as she wants the children to settle down and keep attending their current school. Normality is important to Alice, while Henry is simply annoyed at the risks she is taking.

Leaving to fetch material to board up the broken window, Henry knows he is in a difficult position as he does not want to create an irreparable rift with his daughter. He decides to make the repairs and then offers to pick them up to spend Sunday in Pembroke, with an opportunity for a full family meal. Alice agrees to the invitation and says she will consider the offer to move into Pembroke more permanently, but not just yet.

Returning to her unfinished letter, Alice concludes that there is little point in saying anything about the events of last night. Robert cannot help them from his situation. Why make him worry more.

Chapter 11

The Briefing

12th September 1940, Harwich

Directed to moor up at the near end of Parkeston Quay, the Caithness pulls alongside closest to the harbour entrance and away from the main buildings that form the hub of the base. Soon the news and the evidence of an air raid attack reach the crew. Following the previous night's raid, the shore base buildings of HMS Badger remain intact but there is destruction to mooring pontoons and damage to a few small craft secured at the far end of the long quay.

On deck, the Skipper gives orders to secure the ship and continue with their shore duties while he attempts to find further details of the attack from his visit to HQ. Robert takes the crew through the list of duties that need to be performed during their short stay ashore, while he also tries to calm their nerves over the destruction they see around them. Some of the men are more concerned about their access to the Parkeston village pubs but Robert is sure this is just bluster and a way to conceal their true feelings.

Robert leaves the men and walks along the deck to catch up with the Skipper before he goes ashore.

'Good morning Sir.'

'Good morning Crawford, how are you?'

'Well, thank you, sir.'

'What's on your mind?'

'Well, I'd like to know if you could ask at HQ about our mail delivery.'

'Certainly, I can. Are you busy?'

'Just organising the morning's work, sir,' replies Robert as he suppresses a look of surprise at the question.

'Good. I've just had a signal from the staff at HMS Badger asking me if I can send someone to a briefing to review E-Boat activity. It's being held over in the main building at Parkeston Quay.'

Robert is very glad of something to do instead of the maintenance tasks, so he immediately answers, 'Yes sir, when is this happening?'

'0900 hours. Report to Commander Blake.'

'Aye, sir.' And suddenly Robert's day has improved. He starts to wonder what he will be asked to do as he has never been to a review before, and he does not know what to expect.

Robert strides across the quay to reach the shore station that acts as the HQ for HMS Badger. He managed to have a decent wash in the aft cabin, before putting on his best uniform. His pride in the uniform has grown since it was issued to him and feeling closer to the Patrol Service, he explores where this emotion is coming from. He is surprised when he realises it is coming from his confidence in leading the men.

The shore station is an unimposing building in a quiet part of the larger port. Having asked the navy rating manning the front desk for directions, he finds the right location for the briefing and upon entering a room off the main corridor, he is immediately and warmly greeted by an officer he assumes is Blake.

Robert salutes the officer and Blake responds, 'Good morning, I'm Commander Blake from Nore. Who are you?'

Robert is overwhelmed by the greeting but recovers to make a sensible response, 'Second-Hand Crawford sir, from HMT Caithness.'

'Ah, good to meet you Crawford. I read the report about your recent E-Boat experience and the torpedo that exploded. Lucky escape, eh!'

'Yes, sir.'

'Good, say hello to the others here and then take a seat and we'll start in a short while.'

Robert looks around the room and acknowledges four other patrol servicemen from various ships. He nods and general greetings are exchanged as all the men search for a sign of an officer to salute, but there are none. Robert takes a seat at the big wooden table in the centre of the room. Surprised that Blake has heard of the Caithness's encounter with the torpedo, he begins to wonder more and more about the real purpose of this gathering. After a short while, one other man from the patrol service joins them at the table and then Blake indicates he is ready to start.

'Thank you for coming here this morning gentlemen. I know that for some of you this is part of your well-earned shore stopover, so I'll try to keep this to just the morning. I'm sure you are all wondering why we have asked you here and I hope to explain. You have all had first-hand and close experience of an E-Boat attack, and more importantly, been fired on by a torpedo and survived to tell the tale. Is that correct?'

Looking around the table at each other, the men give general nods indicating that this is the case.

'So, shortly I'm going to ask you to tell the story of your encounter to all gathered here, but first, let me give you some background. All the information I am sharing is classified so you need to be very careful who you pass it on to. Talking to your Skippers is fine.'

Blake explains that E-Boat activity has increased in the North Sea since the Dunkirk rescue. As a result, invasion defence planning is focusing heavily on the E-Boat threat, as there is a high likelihood they will form the main attack force against British destroyers. There is less concern regarding U-Boats as they have been far less effective in the North Sea because of the sandbanks, shallows, and the growing numbers of mines in the East Coast barrier.

British commanders believe the Suffolk coast is an ideal place for an invasion force to land and establish a beachhead, ready to supply troops and equipment moving west towards London. Before landing at the coast, the enemy must first clear a wide corridor through the sea mine barrier and E-Boats are expected to flood through Gap E, attacking British ships as they defend the coastal side of the barrier. Once the risk of defending destroyers is removed, enemy minesweepers can start their task of clearing a larger corridor through to the coast.

Common to the E-Boat and U-Boat threat is their use of the same destructive torpedo. The great advantage the E-Boats have over their prey is their speed, with these deadly craft capable of over forty knots. These fast attack craft can easily run rings around the current auxiliary patrol vessels.

Blake pauses for these specifics to sink in before adding further details that leave those in the room even more shocked. Statistics have been collected over the past three months that show one in three torpedoes are failing and exploding short of their target. Commander Blake explains that they are interested in as much information as they can gather on the torpedoes, hoping they can find a pattern to explain the failure rate. He tells them that the big prize is to determine if there is a way to force the failure rate higher or even overcome the threat completely.

The next stage of the review involves sharing an enormous amount of technical data on the E-Boat's torpedo design and construction. Absorbing the detail, Robert is fascinated to discover that the torpedoes run off compressed air. Many more details of the mechanics are explained as Blake wants to help improve everyone's understanding. Ultimately, it is the detail of the trigger mechanism that holds the key. The trigger is used to detonate the torpedo on impact, although it can also trigger the explosive payload when it detects a change in the surrounding magnetic field, usually caused by a large metal object such as a vessel's hull. The magnetic field switch comes into play when the torpedo is aimed to pass below a ship and detonate directly under its keel. The enormous force of the underwater explosion breaks the back of the ship and increases the chance of it sinking.

Robert immediately thinks back to their recent patrol when they saw an E-Boat up close. Up until this point, he had no notion of what happened that night, but now it seems obvious that the torpedo's trigger mechanism detected the magnetic field change from their hull too early, causing the explosion.

Commander Blake asks the assembled crew members to describe their encounters with E-Boats and Robert listens intently to the other men seated around the table as they tell their stories and provide details that are very similar to his own experience.

A Second-Hand from HMT Powys recalls his narrow escape from an E-Boat attack a few weeks earlier. Detailing the exact moment, he describes how a torpedo was launched and how he was able to track its course through the waves, focusing on the disturbance caused by the screws. He seems most struck by the speed the torpedo reached.

Blake asks the crewman, 'do you think that was just the churning of the water you could see?'

'Well, yes.'

'That's interesting because there is always a stream of bubbles created by the compressed air engine running in the torpedo. Do you think you saw any of those bubbles?'

'I can't be certain, as it happened so quickly. I was standing on the bridge and the light was fading. I saw the E-Boat launch the torpedo from one of its tubes and I was able to follow its track in my binoculars, but I can't be sure if there were bubbles or not.'

'That's fine,' answers Blake in a sympathetic manner to try and help the crewman remember. 'And what happened to the torpedo in your case?'

'Well, it missed us by passing behind the stern. There were only a few feet in it!'

There is a pause where no one comments.

'Thank you for giving us those details. Right, who's next.'

They come to Robert next, and he outlines the contact they had with an E-Boat explaining that he did not see anything until there was a massive explosion roughly fifty yards off the starboard side of the ship.

'That sounds exactly like the situation we have been hearing about. As I mentioned earlier there are clear signs that there is a problem with the torpedo's magnetic detection mechanism, and it appears to be triggering early, possibly in as many as one in three cases.'

'Well, I think that saved us as it exploded fifty yards out and it would certainly have hit us otherwise,' considers Robert.

There is another long pause while everyone takes in the significance of the outcome.

Commander Blake moves the conversation on to its next stage by asking the crewmen if they think there is anything they can do to improve their chances against the E-Boat attacks.

Robert jumps straight in, 'well we can't outrun them or outmanoeuvre them, so we'll have to come up with something clever.'

'Yes, I agree. Any suggestions?'

'Sir, we can shell the boats and keep them under machine-gun fire, but their speed makes them a very hard target. Is there any way we can attack the torpedoes?'

'I like your thinking Crawford. Any ideas on taking out the torpedoes?'

Robert does not want to hog the discussion, so he looks around the table to encourage some other contributions, but none come forth. So, he adds, 'is there a way to force the magnetic detonation early.'

'Please elaborate.'

'The torpedoes are very sensitive in that way and possibly too sensitive. Talking to some of the crews of minesweepers we are "Wiping" ships now to reduce their magnetic field. This is done to stop the ships from setting off the new magnetic mines.

Could we do something like that for torpedoes, but in reverse, and set them off early?'

'Well, yes in theory. This has been suggested and investigated but changing the field to detonate torpedoes early would also do the same for mines. In tests the mines would detonate sooner, but close to the ships, and they would still cause serious damage. Good thinking though. Any more ideas.'

Everyone around the table looks at everyone else, but no more suggestions are made.

The crewman from HMT Powys, who spoke earlier suggests another approach asking, 'what if we had mini-depth charges that we could launch into the path of the torpedo?'

'Another good idea that has been explored. It's a challenge to get the timing right because of the speed the torpedoes are travelling. If you spot a torpedo a hundred yards out from your ship then you've got less than five seconds to react.'

This fact stuns the room into another long silence.

'Gentlemen. Thank you for your time today. Your experiences will help us build a better picture of what is happening out there and then go on towards saving lives.'

With that, the meeting finishes and the men start to make their way through the door.

'Crawford, can I have a quick word,' asks Commander Blake.

Robert turns and joins him at the desk, 'yes, sir.'

'Please don't be despondent. I saw your reaction to some of the discussions we have had, and you did not look happy.'

'Sorry, sir. It is the constant battle against mines and now torpedoes. We need some help.'

'I see. I can't offer anything now, but we have a lot of people working on ways to help you. Please be encouraged.'

'Thank you, sir.'

Walking back to his ship he thinks about all that is being asked of the patrol crews. He challenges himself to remain positive when he speaks to the crew of the Caithness as he must be the voice of calm and reason.

Climbing onboard he sees the Skipper in the wardroom doorway and is unable to avoid a conversation he would rather have had later in the day. Robert is invited into the wardroom and is asked to take a seat.

'How did your briefing go?' asks the Skipper in a very friendly manner.

'Good sir. Yes, it was good. Lots of useful information and lots to think about.'

'Well fill me in then.'

Robert recounts the technical details they were given on the torpedo, the sightings described by the other men, and eventually the discussion of possible countermeasures.

'Sounds very interesting. What should we change?'

'Well, I'm still feeling overwhelmed by the dangers we face. I think we have been very lucky so far as roughly one in three torpedoes trigger early. That is what happened to us.'

'I see. So, you don't think it could have been a mine. You think the explosion was a torpedo as we guessed when it happened.'

'Yes sir. From what we heard today I think the E-Boat we met managed to get a torpedo into the water and it detonated early.'

'That is fascinating. Are there any new approaches we should be taking?'

'No sir. We should still be targeting the E-Boats with as much firepower as we can. That's how we will survive.'

'You say survive, Crawford. That's an interesting choice of words to describe our situation, don't you think.'

'Well, sir. That's how I see it.'

'Look Crawford, let's cut the "sir" out here and let's talk more like men. We're in harbour after all. I know you are a very experienced seaman and I'm skipper because I'm a reservist. I appreciate all that you have been doing to make this crew work together and they are starting to look good working the watches. You should be pleased with that.'

'Thank you. I'm pleased with the way the men are pulling together.'

'Good, you are a natural leader and I've seen it from day one. Tell me more about where you are from.'

Robert is surprised by this but tells the Skipper of his Scottish roots and the family he now has back in Wales. He talks of his time at sea and the comfort it brings him. Then he does something that he immediately regrets as he realises it may cause offence. He asks, 'how did you come to be here?'

There is a small pause where Robert starts to stiffen in his seat, but he need not have worried as Robinson responds with a friendly smile, 'Well, much like you, I grew up by the sea in Cornwall. We lived in Torpoint and my father was in the navy and based out of Devonport. We did everything connected with the sea as children and then my father served in the Great War.'

'Did he come through that?'

'Yes, he then spent his remaining years shore-based and retired a few years ago.'

'You've got the navy in your blood then.'

'Yes, I joined the merchant navy in 1925, at the age of sixteen, and then I saw a lot of the world.'

'You're the same age as me then as I went off to sea with my father in 1925.'

'Yes, I must be.'

'How did you end up at the Nest.'

'Well, I signed up to the Royal Naval Reserve a few years ago as I thought it might be a good way into the navy. Being in the reserves meant I was called up back in October.'

The two men chat for a while longer and speak of their families and how they have left them at home. Robert is surprised at how much he is warming to the Skipper, now they have had time to talk. That is a big challenge on board as men are working the watches or resting, and it is only the times in port that allow good conversations to happen. Robert makes his excuses and starts to leave the wardroom.

'Before you go, Crawford, I'm still a bit concerned by what you said earlier especially about how we need to survive. Do you see us as trying to survive this war?'

'I see us trying to survive each patrol. The E-Boats are deadly, and we are a slow-moving, easy to hit, target.'

'It's not like you to be pessimistic.'

'I won't be in front of the men, but I think we need to work hard at the weapons as that's our only real chance in all of this.'

'Thank you for your honesty, Crawford. I'll take your views seriously. I'm about to meet with the base commander at HQ and get more details of last night's air raid. I'll update you later.'

The men part and Robert immediately feels he has overdone the negativity. He wants to be honest with the Skipper and not sugar coat things, but his current mood of isolation and frustration is showing through. His conversation with the Skipper has helped him to get to know him better and this was long overdue. Something is still puzzling him as he cannot understand how such an intelligent and experienced man can be a great Skipper but misses out by not communicating well with the crew. The crew think he is aloof, and he does little to persuade them otherwise.

Pondering many things, Robert realises he cannot wait to be back at sea, despite believing they are a slow-moving, easy target for the enemy.

Chapter 12

The Raid

12th September 1940 – Harwich

It is late afternoon and the crew have worked hard to replenish the ship. Returning from HQ, the Skipper asks Robert to join him in the wardroom for what is now their familiar routine when matters need to be discussed in private.

'Well Crawford, Command is certainly shocked by what happened here last night. It seems to have taken them completely by surprise.'

'Do you have any more details, sir?'

'Yes, the raid started just after 2200 hours. A number of Heinkel bombers came over the town, not dropping anything on the old town, but deliberately targeting HMS Badger facilities and Parkeston Quay itself.'

'Were there any fatalities?'

'One fatality, and some serious injuries caused by blast damage and flying glass. No major ship damage despite there being two destroyers anchored off the quay when the bombers came over.'

'So, was this a deliberate attack on the base?'

'Yes, no doubt about it. I've just spoken with a senior officer and there is a general feeling that the enemy has upped their game and that there will be more air attacks on North Sea patrols and our ports. Command believes this is a run-up to an invasion and Churchill's speech yesterday was designed to prepare the country for that eventuality. There is plenty of intelligence for this, as well as the rhetoric coming from Berlin.'

'Does this change our orders?'

'No, not for the time being. We're to rest up here for our normal shore leave today and be back on patrol in the morning. But the raid last night caught them out, so I am expecting that we will be asked to fully man the ship at all times.'

'I see, so no shore leave. That will please the men.'

'I know but we should wait for specific new orders on that before we let the men know. I'll fill you in as soon as I know. Carry on Crawford.'

'Aye, sir.'

This situation leaves Robert thinking about the best way forward should there be another air raid. He has not considered an attack while in harbour and does not know if they should move back out to sea or remain at the quayside. He does not know if they should open fire on the bombers or leave that to other defences that surround the harbour. Realising there are too many questions he decides it is best to work with the Skipper's orders once they arrive. The crew want information but all he can do is confirm the air raid details and say he is awaiting orders. Any situation is challenging when the crew have a sense they are not being told the full details. In the military, only rumours are left to fill the void.

Robert takes some time away from the Caithness to visit some of the other ships currently in harbour. He wants to hear from the other second-hands and experienced crewmen, checking if there is any news to be heard or if there are any tall tales of recent adventures at sea. There is a serious side to this as he often learns of useful pieces of information regarding RNPS operations or possible new tactics of the enemy. It reminds him of sharing information with other trawlermen, but it was different then as there was competition to consider. You always shared details of anything safety-related or information that could help the wellbeing of the fishermen, but there was nothing given away that would help other trawlers get a better catch or return the fish for an early sale. Commercial fishing is a tough business and there is a fine line between offering genuine help and keeping a competitive edge where you can.

Learning from the other crews, Robert knows that patrols are getting busier with the heightened enemy presence along the whole seacoast. He does learn that there are many more mines being dropped by enemy planes but only in certain areas. This makes sense as any sea assault plans would need to have clear routes to the coast. He hopes this pattern is obvious to those in command.

Returning to his ship he notices that the Skipper is back on board, so he makes his way directly to the wardroom and knocks on the door.

'Come in.'

'I saw you were back onboard sir and I wondered if there were any new orders?'

'Yes, come in and sit down. There are a few things to consider. Command is expecting another raid tonight as they believe the one last night was a simple test of air defences by only three bombers. Intelligence reports suggest that the main aim of the attacks is to disable the quay's refuelling capability. Without a refuelling base, the fleet protecting the North Sea will be paralysed and the defences against an attacking sea force will be gravely depleted.'

'That is serious.'

'Yes, and that's not all. We know aeroplanes have been dropping mines close to the harbour mouth but there were also mines dropped past the harbour entrance last night.'

'But that means we could have hit one of them on our way in this morning.'

'Yes, it does. As a result, the sweeping activities have been increased and the deep-water sections of the harbour and rivers are being prioritised as we speak.'

'Good, that's a relief! Sorry Skipper that wasn't meant to sound so sarcastic.'

'Yes, that also affects the plans should there be a raid this evening. Because of the danger of dropped mines, they are currently sweeping the harbour channels and its entrance so large ships can leave their anchorages and go to sea. This includes any destroyers in port. All remaining ships are to provide firepower and defend the quay against enemy aircraft, provided they can be clearly identified.'

'Very well sir. Those orders are clear.'

'Yes, please take the time to explain them to the crew and ensure they know we will call action stations if necessary, but they must wait for the direct order to open fire.'

'Yes, sir. Understood.'

'Good, carry on Crawford.'

'Aye, sir.'

Robert makes his way through the ship and speaks to the crew explaining their orders and what to expect that evening. It is important to know that the normal sea-based watches will operate, and the Skipper's team is covering the first watch. He spends some time with the engine room men who are on cleaning duties, to discover if they could be of help during action stations as the ship will not be under power. They conclude that the best way to help is by providing extra support to get ammunition ready for the guns. The shells and powder charges are kept in lockers on both sides of the foc'sle. This is convenient for the main 12-pounder gun, but Brown must do a heroic job of feeding the ammunition from the lockers to Altman who is loading the gun. If we could arrange some more help in that way, then the firing rate of the gun is sure to increase. Thomas speaks for those in the engine room and assures

Robert that the two stokers and himself will help in whatever way they can.

The quay at Parkeston is long and the Caithness has moored a considerable distance from the main HQ building and the fuel stores. This provides some comfort in the lead up to another raid, but Robert is concerned about being alongside when bombs are falling and the quay itself is the target. He knows their guns are more effective if the ship is stable, but he feels there is natural protection in this harbour and the ship would be reasonably stable anchored off a buoy in the channel.

At 1800 hours the whole crew gather for a good meal, with the start of the second dog watch delayed allowing all the men to come together and share their food. Despite no shore leave the men are in good spirits and they seem more relaxed than when at sea. The first watch starts at 2000 hours and everyone is commenting on the odd feeling there is as they anticipate an air attack in this way. Robert is in the wheelhouse with the Skipper and Harris is on the bridge as lookout. Fredericks is there as a helmsman but in these circumstances, he is asked to use his lookout skills with Harris.

The watch continues without any sign of activity until just after 2230 hours when the sky is lit up by searchlights from Landguard Fort. Sitting on a spit of land that stretches out into the North Sea, the fort makes a natural defence for the harbour. Searchlights highlight the enemy aircraft and soon the fort's anti-aircraft guns open fire, trying to stop the bombers before they reach the quay.

Action stations are called, and the men take their positions. Destroyers have left the port and that is right, even though their firepower would have been a great help. Robert estimates that there are six converted trawlers in port with other ships either out on patrol or sent out to sea for their own protection.

Only the Skipper and Robert are in the wheelhouse when the CO decides to confide in the second-hand.

'Command has obviously received some intelligence that made them sure this raid was happening tonight. All navy ships have been sent to sea and we have been volunteered to help protect HMS Badger headquarters and the facilities here.'

'I see sir. Makes sense when you look at the bigger picture.'

'You don't sound convinced Crawford. We can't talk now so let's discuss this later. Let's join the lookouts and make a decision on these bombers.'

The men move out onto the bridge and join Harris and Fredericks.

'What do we think?' asks the Skipper.

'Looking at them in the searchlights they appear to be Heinkel He 111s and I'd say twelve plus,' adds Harris.

'Let's open fire when they are in range,' announces the Skipper.

'Wait!' exclaims Robert as he suddenly realises they are too close to Harwich and Felixstowe to be launching shells from the 12-Pounder into the air. 'We are aiming at aircraft travelling towards us. Based on where we are moored, if we miss, the shells will come down too close to the town for comfort.'

'What can we do?' asks the Skipper.

'We can open fire with the Lewis guns, but we'll just have to wait to use the main gun until the bombers are closer to us,' responds Robert as he gives the order for the machine guns to open fire.

A nervous time passes before Robert checks with the Skipper and then gives the order to open fire with the 12-Pounder.

The guns fire on the Heinkel bombers coming in on a low-level precision bombing run. The anti-aircraft guns from Landguard Fort have some impact on the bombers but most are getting through. All converted trawlers are now firing at the bombers, but they are a very difficult target based on their altitude.

Firing continues at a tremendous rate, as the bombs start falling, with many explosions erupting in the water and on the land surrounding the quay. A few bombers are damaged by the firing, but the bombs keep falling until the Heinkels pass over and have finished delivering their payload.

The operation of the guns is impressive, as the crew manages to focus on the difficult and dangerous conditions. With no time to think, the metronomic process of loading and firing is hypnotic to those watching. Elsewhere on the Caithness, men are watching the action unfold as each explosion brings its own terror. The men have no experience of such a concentrated attack, and it shakes everyone's bones. The vision of terror is burning their eyes, the sound is splitting their eardrums and the percussive force hits their bodies like a sledgehammer. Praying for the horror to stop, they all hope to survive the next few minutes. An explosion erupts close to the trawler and the heat sears against their exposed skin. Debris falls on the ship and the collective belief is they will not go unharmed if the next bomb falls closer.

As suddenly as the raid started, they are now left with only the sounds of their own guns. A cease-fire order is given and the crew stand assessing the destruction. It is hard to tell the full extent in the darkness, but a few people are attempting to put out fires that have started on pontoons and in small supply buildings. Small fires take time to come under control, but it is quickly understood that the oil tanks, pumping facilities and solid fuel stores are all undamaged.

Standing down the crew allows the men to return to a state of normal operation and they can recover from the raid as best as they can. Speaking with the men, Robert thanks them for their brave response to the attack. He organises tasks for the watches for the rest of the night and hopes many of the men can get some rest. Speaking to the Skipper he realises just how much the senior man is shocked by the assault. There is nothing to say to him but leave him to the solitude of the wardroom.

First thing in the morning it is easier to establish the damage to the quay and port area. They have been very fortunate to receive only minor damage, mostly caused by debris from the explosions close by. The minesweepers are already hard at work, clearing the channels of mines dropped last night. Rifle shots ring out across the calm waterfront as mines are sunk.

Suddenly, a whistle sounds and there is shouting just off the concrete section of the quay. The Skipper and Robert start to leave the ship via the gangway when they are stopped by a navy rating. He tells them there is an unexploded bomb close to their ship and that they must move to the other end of the quay immediately. The men return to the deck and order the crew to start the engine and get the ship moving. But Robert knows the engines cannot be started that quickly. Boilers were fired up at the start of the morning watch as steam needs to be raised slowly. They are halfway through the watch and there are another two hours to go until they were expecting to leave port. There is a general concern for the ship and the men do not want to leave it to potential destruction.

Robert looks out on the water and sees a minesweeper returning to the quay. He quickly finds Bowes in the wireless room and asks him to signal the minesweeper to help tow them away from the danger. Bowes reminds him they need the minesweepers name, so Robert finds his binoculars and reads off the name from the ship's bow. The signal asks for urgent help as there is an unexploded bomb close to the Caithness and she needs to be moved before her boiler is ready.

Responding quickly, the minesweeper approaches and the crew help attach a tow line from the bow of the Caithness to the rear bollards on the towing vessel. They cast off lines and slowly the Caithness is pulled away from the danger area and is towed to a new position at the opposite end of the long quay. Fortunately, there is enough steam to allow the steering gear to function, and as a result the towing operation proceeds quickly. Everyone is relieved by how smoothly this manoeuvre was carried out and Robert suddenly wonders why they didn't just leave the ship moored where it was and evacuate the crew until the bomb was dealt with. The men reacted naturally to save their ship, and this is down to them not wanting the enemy to deprive them of their means to fight back.

Once the Caithness is moored up again Robert leaves to find out what is happening. He meets a navy rating who is guarding the safety area. The rating tells him that they have their own disposal team based at HMS Badger so there should be no problem finding the right people to deal with this. However, it could be some time before the quay is fully operational again. The rating does not know of any reported damage to the refuelling systems, so Robert returns to the Caithness to send a signal to find out how their current stay in port is impacted. The exchange of signals with Command shows that they can leave at their designated time of 0800.

Robert approaches the wardroom and sees a light inside. Knocking on the door he is not sure if he should be disturbing the Skipper at this time. His knock is answered by a friendly, 'come in.'

'Good morning sir.'

'Come in Crawford. Please make yourself comfortable.'

'Thank you, sir. We'll be ready to depart at 0800.'

'Yes, I'm glad we can get back to patrol. Are the men ready?'

'Yes, they're ready. We'll run the watches to continue from last night.'

'I'd much rather be at sea than confined to the port. What do you think Crawford?'

'I'm with you, sir. I'd much rather be at sea and be able to defend ourselves. The biggest difference then is we would be a much smaller target. We're part of a much bigger area to defend here.'

'What do you make of all of this talk of invasion plans and what Hitler is saying about us being defeated?'

'Well, since France was lost we seem to be the next in line and Hitler won't stop until he gets what he wants. The talk amongst the men is all about what will happen to their families if enemy forces land ashore. They expect the worst and that is what keeps them fighting.'

'There isn't much time left before the plan will become obvious. We have seen what happened here to try to damage the supply links. It's all about softening us up.'

'I think you are right, but I think we have some fight left in us yet. Have you managed to catch up with the senior staff here?'

'Yes, between the mayhem I've spent some time understanding how our patrols can be strengthened in the coming weeks.'

'That sounds encouraging.'

'Yes it is but I can't give you any details yet as the orders have not been finalised. But I expect we'll know soon.'

The men continue to talk until they hear the eight bells signalling the start of the forenoon watch. Hurrying to the wheelhouse they set about their task of going to sea. The next patrol awaits.

Chapter 13

Invasion Plans

13th September 1940, North Sea

Patrols are running at an increased level each month since the end of Operation Dynamo. Hitler is making speeches that stress the likelihood of a land assault and these are backed up by photo reconnaissance details of his plans to overcome Britain. Hitler plans to force Britain into a negotiated surrender, but the British government is not interested in negotiating and do not believe an invasion will succeed.

The Battle of Britain is growing in intensity, and since early July the Luftwaffe are focusing their attacks on ports and shipping along all stretches of the coast. Specifically, the RNPS is reacting to a pronounced increase in attacks on shipping in the southern North Sea and to bombing raids on ports in the same area.

Britain has a new and secret technology, designed to help with the early warning of enemy aircraft formations as they approach the coast. This vital new technology, called Radio Detection Finding, fits in well with the manual control systems developed by RAF fighter command which efficiently scrambles Spitfires and Hurricanes to meet Luftwaffe attacks. RDF is a supremely well-guarded secret, and little is known of the string of stations positioned along the British coast, including two in Suffolk, at Bawdsey and Darsham. Very few people are aware of the importance of the constructions that resemble large wireless masts. These structures are vital to the war effort and must be protected.

At the start of the next patrol Robert's head is full of stories from their last stay ashore. Newspaper articles and discussions at Parkeston Harbour mirror many conversations across the country. The common theme in these stories is the probable offensive attack against Britain, and it is causing tension for everyone. Robert sees the situation from a different angle as he believes there is a job to be done to stop the invasion and protect the country. Absorbed in his own job, he acknowledges that he must lead the crew and keep their tensions in mind. One of his challenges is dealing with stories that have been shared about the risks to families from an invading army. Circulating rumours have everyone on edge, as men's imaginations run riot with the thoughts of what might happen to their loved ones at the hands of the enemy. Family separation makes the situation worse as the lack of news and little contact makes the men restless. Some men are not married but they have close family. The reality today is that there is a patrol schedule to manage, and they must act as one vital cog in the machinery needed to repel the enemy.

Steaming out of Harwich harbour, the Caithness joins four other trawlers and a Destroyer, HMS Mentmore.

The extra trawler, and the inclusion of a destroyer, demonstrate the seriousness given to new patrol patterns. Returning to their familiar patrol, the Caithness is covering a sector from the Aldeburgh Light Ship to a point just south of Dunwich. Their sector has the code letters HW indicating that it is one of a sequence of sectors under the direction of Harwich control. Three other trawlers are covering the sectors to the south of the Caithness and they are designated HT, HU and HV respectively. This patrol has an extra trawler to accommodate, and the plan is to split the HW sector into two, namely HW1 and HW2. Taking HW1, the Caithness covers the northernmost of the two HW sectors, and Robert realises now that there is only a five nautical mile distance for them to cover before turning to patrol the reverse route. HMT Flintshire takes the HW2 sector and is the vessel the Caithness will have the most contact with. The captain of the destroyer is the overall group leader for this patrol.

'This area off the coast of Dunwich is very sensitive, Crawford. I've got some details I can share with you later but for now, I'll just say there is vital equipment in this area of the coast.'

'I see, sir. What about the destroyer? We've not patrolled with one before.'

'I see it as extra strength for patrols while there is a threat of invasion. The destroyer is meant to cover all the sectors from HT in the south to us and then back again. What have you heard, Crawford?'

'I haven't heard anything Skipper.'

'Carry on Crawford,' commands the Skipper as he leaves Robert leading the remainder of the forenoon watch.

'Aye, sir,' responds Robert as the Skipper is halfway out of the door to the wheelhouse.

Robert checks their course and speed as they head north to the top limit of their HW1 patrol. Before the turn, he quickly grabs his binoculars to scan the coast as he is curious about the equipment mentioned in his last conversation with the Skipper. It does not take him long to locate four tall wireless masts approximately four miles inland from the coast. Robert makes a note of the mast's position relative to the coastguard station near Dunwich as he wants to check the significance of the masts on their new patrol configuration. Soon they are at the northernmost extent of their patrol and in the distance they see the craft from the Lowestoft FZ sector travelling south towards them. After the turn, and partway down their sector, they pass the destroyer heading north on their port side. Creating an inspiring sight, he hopes the crew see the warship and that it makes them feel a little safer. He welcomes the added protection based on the increase in enemy contact they have seen over the past few weeks.

Leading the first watch that evening, Robert has his binoculars fixed to his eyes as he pans from side to side in search of sea and air activity. The sky has darkened significantly following the 1920 hours sunset and since then the only help for lookouts has been the light cast by the half-moon. At 2210 hours the ship's bell signals action stations and the crew hurry to their customary positions. The Skipper joins Robert and they discuss the sighting. 'What have you got?'

'E-Boats coming from the east. I can see two boats on a course level with our position and scanning around I can see two other boats travelling east but south of us, sir.'

'We need to telegraph this to the rest of the patrol, and specifically to the group leader on the destroyer. Open fire when in range.'

Robert joins Slater on the bridge and shouts the order, 'open fire to the starboard side when targets are in range.'

Confirmations come back from the gunners as the Skipper joins them and announces, 'E-Boats are attacking all boats in the patrol.'

'The boats heading for us are splitting up!' shouts Slater as the men on the bridge look to the east. 'The left-most boat has turned north and appears to be trying to get ahead of us.'

'Slater, you track the one heading north, and we'll focus on the one still coming towards us,' as the 12-Pounder opens fire with a ranging shot.

Soon the E-Boat is in range of the Lewis gun as it continues to come under more fire from the trawler's 12-Pounder. Many shots are fired in succession and there is a flash of an explosion as the E-Boat is hit on its starboard side above the waterline. Immediately slowing, the E-Boat returns fire with its machine guns, as its crew scrambles to save it from going ablaze and ultimately sinking. Very gradually the E-Boat turns and heads back towards the east and the trawler crew feels elated by a successful defence of their patrol.

'Slater, what's happened to that other E-Boat?'

'She's slowed, so her wake is harder to track but I think she's heading in a big circle to come around on our port side and start heading to the south. Can you see the wake three points off the port bow?'

'Got it,' exclaims Robert and soon the Skipper has the path too. They track the boat into the night, realising that it will soon be out of range. The Skipper gives the order to break from their patrol and follow the E-Boat. He asks Robert to get signals away to the other patrol vessels, explaining their plans to follow the rogue boat. The other vessels signal back that the combined attack has stopped, with E-Boats turning east and eventually disappearing. Everyone is in a heightened state of alertness as the current situation does not make sense to many of the crew, especially as they have been performing the same patrol duties for weeks. Now there is a significant change. Currently, the Skipper is the only person who knows the scope of their new orders and he is finding it difficult to let Robert in on the details while the current situation unfolds. The other patrol Skippers know the alternative plans that need to be enacted when one other ship goes off patrol and they are quick to respond. HMT Flintshire takes over the full ten nautical miles of the HW sector.

The helm is instructed to turn to port to follow the E-Boat being tracked by Slater. At their current speed of ten knots, the converted trawler would not normally be able to keep up with the enemy vessel. However, the E-Boat is using a slow speed tactic to reduce its wake, and this allows the trawler to maintain a safe following distance. Moving between the bridge and wheelhouse, Robert is able to check that the helmsman is aware of what is happening and also to help him follow the instructions that are coming via the lookout. While in the wheelhouse he checks the charts to establish their current position and course, and to ensure there are no upcoming obstacles or surprises. The enemy craft is following a course that takes them towards Southwold and Robert is still none the wiser regarding their new orders and the activity currently playing out in front of them. As they successfully track the enemy vessel there is an opportunity for the Skipper to take Robert to the wardroom and outline their orders.

'We're in a new situation, Crawford. I mentioned this when we were back in Parkeston Quay following the bombing raid. Command at Harwich has given us the role of providing extra protection for this area of the coast. That is why we doubled up on the HW sector so that one vessel could peel off and provide intelligence reports on anything happening off the normal patrol.'

'What about the destroyer, sir.'

'Well, most patrols now include destroyers because of the heightened possibility of enemy activity. But the destroyers cannot venture as close to the coast as we can with our draft.'

'Fine. What is so special about this area that means we can steer off course and follow the enemy?'

'Well, I mentioned the coast of Dunwich. There is a critical wireless station inland from Dunwich near the village of Darsham. I think tonight's full E-Boat attack was a diversionary attack to allow the boat we're following to get around to the coast. The enemy was expecting us to stay on our normal patrol course as we have become very predictable. Let's get back up to the wheelhouse as I expect that E-Boat is about to turn south and hug the coast to Dunwich.'

'Aye, sire,' responds a concerned Robert, knowing the wireless station is there from his earlier search, but he still does not understand its significance as he thinks the change to operational orders is an extraordinary reaction.

Returning to the bridge the Skipper and Robert ask Slater for a report on the E-Boat's course and progress.

'Steady on its current course, heading for Southwold, sir.'

'I see. I expect it to turn south soon. Watch out for a turn.'

'Aye, sir.'

'We must cut our lights, Crawford.'

'But surely not the navigation lights, sir?'

'Yes, the navigation lights as well. I know this is a dangerous step to take.'

'Aye, sir.'

'Crawford let's have a look at the charts,' says the Skipper and they both enter the wheelhouse. The movement around the ship is mostly done by the light of the limited moon, but once in the wheelhouse touch and familiarity take over. Robert searches for a torch that has already had its lens covered in masking tape and uses it to retrieve the chart they want to study.

Slater leans in through the wheelhouse door and says, 'They're slowing down sir.'

'Are they turning?'

'No sir, still on the same course.'

'I don't understand this Crawford, where are they heading and why.'

'I don't know sir.'

Studying the charts, they wonder what they have missed and what is it at Southwold that would attract such attention.

Suffolk is an ideal landing location for any force, with its shallow beaches and sparsely populated flat terrain behind the coast. Defences have been organised to repel enemy forces, but no thought has been given to detect individual covert operations that might be planning to land. The E-Boat currently being tracked is part of an elaborate plan to deliver special forces for a raid on the RDF station at Darsham. The enemy knows of the RDF technology but so far attempts to bomb the towers have been relatively unsuccessful. As air attacks grow there is a need to destroy RDF stations and create a gap in the coverage. Such a gap creates a corridor into London and reduces the RAFs capability to intercept bombers before they cross the channel.

Enemy plans for this covert raid include the combined E-Boat raid that started the encounter and also the lone vessel now being tracked towards Southwold. The combined E-Boat raid was designed to maximise confusion within the patrol and to allow the solo raiding craft to slip through undetected. There are many elements to this raid that are not yet apparent to Robert or his patrol crew.

The Skipper, Second-Hand and lookout are outside on the bridge, binoculars fixed to their eyes, maintaining visual contact with the E-Boat that has slowed to only a few knots. A good communication chain from the Skipper to the helmsman, and onwards to the engine room, helps maintain a safe distance and avoid detection by the boat ahead. Robert raises the question, 'Why have they slowed so much, what are they waiting for.'

'I don't know. It's puzzling!' replies the Skipper as they continue to shadow the E-Boat's movements.

Without notice, they are alerted to an air raid warning to the north of Southwold with the customary siren sounding and searchlights from the town hunting for the aerial attackers. Explosions are heard across the calm water as it soon becomes clear to Robert that there is a track of bombs falling across the seafront of the town as a single bomber travels south along the coast. The significance of this attack is not immediately obvious to him as Southwold is not a major target when compared to the ports of Harwich or Lowestoft. A stream of bombs continues to fall, and explosions erupt as the destruction follows the coastline. Is this the start of them softening up the coastal defences?'

'Could be,' answers Slater in a cursory manner. 'I'm still not sure what this E-Boat is doing and why it's still slowly approaching the coast. What's it up to?'

Robert pounces on an idea, 'They're waiting for the bombing to finish before they continue to their destination and I think I know where they're heading. Let me check the charts.'

Robert returns and announces, 'They're heading for the river Blyth. Skipper, I think the bombing is a distraction.'

'No. They wouldn't go to all this trouble to simply get into the Blyth River. There's nothing there, and the entrance is guarded by the army.'

'That's what the attack is for Skipper, to make everyone on the ground think about the bombing of the town, and nothing else.'

Responding to Robert's theory, the E-Boat steers to starboard to approach the mouth of the Blyth from the south, before hugging the coast and moving north at a reduced speed. All three men on the bridge follow the manoeuvre and see the lights of the enemy vessel disappear as it turns quietly to port and passes through the river entrance.

'Let's get closer,' orders the Skipper and Robert relays the command to the helm and to the engine room. Staying in the wheelhouse Robert oversees the steps needed as they get closer to the mouth of the Blyth River. Keeping the trawler at a distance that will avoid discovery, he is also conscious that they are running without any lights and they could easily have a collision with other enemy craft in the vicinity.

The silhouette of the E-Boat passes through the mouth of the river and goes unchallenged as the focus for the coastal defence soldiers is drawn away from the river to the destruction in town and possible enemy landings on the beaches. Anyone observing the E-Boat as it moves into the river from the Walberswick bank would assume it was a British motor torpedo boat, as no markings or flags are being flown. British MTBs are a familiar sight along these shores since the formation of Coastal Forces at the start of the year.

Robert reappears and recommends, 'Skipper, we should call this into Harwich, but first we should set ourselves up to block the river and cut off the E-Boat's return.'

'Agreed,' is the simple and muted response as Robert believes he has overstepped the mark and should be making recommendations and not trying to force his plans on the Skipper.

Deciding this is not the time to work out any differences in approach, he instructs the gun crews on the plans and passes details onto the helmsman, leaving no one in any doubt. His next task is to visit the wireless room and send a signal to Harwich, but the Skipper intervenes and leaves Robert certain of who is notifying F.O.I.C. of any developments in their unfamiliar patrol pattern.

Soon they are entering the mouth of the river and there is no sign of the E-Boat. The mouth of the Blyth acts as the harbour for Southwold and the tides can cause strong currents and make it difficult to manoeuvre a vessel such as the Caithness. Stanford is at the helm and he needs all of the skills he has developed to cope with the currents.

The chart indicates a left-hand bend in a mile as the Blyth takes its course inland. After a further mile, there are more bends in the river as it continues to meander its way to the north of the village of Blythburgh. Robert is convinced the E-Boat is planning to land undercover troops as far inland as they can, leaving a short cross-country trek to their target. He is no military tactician but looking at the maps of this area it is obvious to him that the river is the best way to remain undetected and get close to the Darsham wireless masts. Providing textbook cover for the E-Boat, the river allows the special forces troops to get back on board within two hours, and an opportunity to head for the open sea before anyone has detected them.

The Skipper returns from the wireless room in a confident frame of mind as Harwich have commended him for their actions and commanded him to stop the E-Boat from getting back to sea at any cost. The army defending the area have been told of the enemy's actions. Robert outlines his theory of the raid that is planned on the Wireless Masts and the Skipper takes no time to send another signal to update Harwich on the progress of the enemy craft and its ultimate target. Their discovery and their actions are likely to stand them well, but there is still a lot of work to do as the pressure is now on them to complete the defensive task they have set themselves.

Having alerted army command, the target can be protected, but the challenge they face on the Caithness is based on the progress the enemy makes. If the army can intercept the enemy craft at Blythburgh, before the troops have alighted, then the boat is likely to try and escape at high speed, even under fire. If the troops have already landed then there is likely to be an exchange of fire and the mission may be abandoned. In these circumstances, there will be a retreat and the E-Boat may or may not wait for the troops. Whichever way they look at it the men of the Caithness are now expecting the E-Boat to try to escape past their ship within the hour.

Robert turns the ship's lights on, so they are identifiable to anyone on the shore. He moves about the ship giving an update to the crew, also explaining the logistics of their situation. He quickly visits the engine and boiler room not to leave them out of the plans as he always thinks those stuck below decks are the last to know what is happening. Thomas thanks him for the information and he also encourages him to be confident in his plans. The support lifts Robert and it allows him to smile just as

Altman chips in with a stream of expletives aimed at the enemy.

Robert's next priority is to contact the army ashore to get the defences manned again to focus more firepower on the returning E-Boat. He notices they can bring the ship alongside at a harbour wall just inside the mouth of the river, so he arranges to moor up and goes looking for anyone from the army. He is fortunate and finds a sergeant who has returned to the Southwold bank of the river. Robert takes his time to explain the situation in detail and the army man assures him they will have the defences on the side of the river manned and covering the waterway in minutes. Robert also asks if the army have enough men to send a detachment to the first bend in the river and set up a firing position as the E-Boat first comes into sight. The sergeant does not know if he can arrange this but says he will get a message to his HQ and pass on the request.

Returning to the Caithness, Robert repositions it in the middle of the river, where it slightly narrows, and there is an equal gap between the banks. Ahead of them, there is a straight nine-hundred-yard stretch of river that the E-Boat must enter as it tries to return to the sea. This is perfect for the plan Robert has in mind, as he intends to turn the ship sideways across the river to reduce the space the E-Boat could use to pass on each side. Using this approach, he can reduce the gap for the passing boat to thirty-five feet on either side and with the depth severely reduced at each bank there would be no escape.

Suddenly, he stops dead in his tracks as a huge realisation hits him. The length of river available to the E-Boat when they first see his ship is easily enough distance to launch torpedoes and blow them out of the water. Re-evaluating quickly, Robert goes back to his plan to positioning the ship head on to the oncoming E-Boat, minimising the target area for any torpedoes they manage to launch. In this configuration, there is still a huge onus on the gun crew to disable the E-Boat as soon as it appears. This requires the crew to reach a firing rate that is better than the best they have achieved so far. The success of this encounter comes down to how many obstacles the enemy crew expect to be in their way as they reach the straight stretch of the river. If they are travelling as fast as they can in the restricted navigation channels then they may not be immediately thinking of how to quickly launch torpedoes. They are sure to have their guns manned and there is no way of hiding from the E-Boat's twenty-millimetre canon once it starts to unload shells towards them.

Remembering to report back to the Skipper, Robert explains his plans as it is easy to keep thinking he is the skipper, especially as he prioritises the safety of the men. In this case, the ship's CO is happy with all the preparations Robert has made and both men seem relieved there is a plan in place.

'What do you think our chances are?' asks Slater, as the three men are back together again at the front of the bridge. Robert keeps quiet and the Skipper responds, 'I'd say we are in the best position given the E-Boat is fleeing and they may not be thinking about anything but escaping the river. What do you say Crawford?'

'I agree, Skipper. This depends on how prepared they are when they see us. We must put her out of action before she has a chance to sinks us. It's a simple case of us versus them.'

Everyone is focused on the time they have been in position and how soon the enemy will arrive. Robert does not expect a warning from any army engagement with the enemy close to the RDF target. He believes it is too much to expect a signal from the soldier's contact with the enemy to get through the army's chain of command and back out through Harwich.

Time passes slowly as the crew remain steadfast in their places as they focus all their attention on one spot further up the river. Suddenly, gunfire in the distance alerts them to the position of the E-Boat before it appears around the bend in the river. Army rifles and a machine gun are opening fire from the right-hand bank as seen from the ship. Robert is encouraged as he thinks back to the hurried conversation he had with the army sergeant and how he had hoped for the support they were now providing. Any fire the army can lay down at this stage will have a huge bearing on the next few minutes. The hope is that the E-Boat's Skipper is distracted enough to flee the firing and not detect the trawler guarding the river mouth.

Accelerating hard coming out of the bend, the enemy craft is rapidly returning fire to the soldiers on the bank. Soon the E-Boat is heading down the river, shaking off the gunfire now at its rear. Difficult to detect at first, those on the trawler's bridge gradually notice that the E-Boat is accelerating towards them unimpeded. The boat is now fully visible with bright lights facing forward as they have given up their shadowy progress as it is impossible to navigate the river without their forward-facing lights.

The 12-Pounder gun crew have been given clear orders to open fire as soon as the boat appears, and they waste no time in getting their shells away. The Lewis guns on the side of the bridge open fire and use tracer ammunition to illuminate the distance to the enemy craft. Shelling from the 12-Pounder is impressive and a further improvement on the rate of fire achieved in downing the Heinkel. As everyone relives the experience of the bomber closing on them, there is a quick realisation that the odds of this ending as well are shortening fast.

The men on the bridge look down the waterway and each one wills the shells to find their target as the gap closes. Robert is fixed on the E-Boat's progress as it is bombarded with fire. The canon on the front of the E-Boat starts to find its target and suddenly the men outside the wheelhouse feel very exposed. However, they do not move and continue to operate their guns rooted to the spot. The bravery of the men is exemplary and is key to the outcome of this exchange.

Robert's greatest fear becomes reality as the E-Boat manages to launch a single torpedo at a distance of four hundred yards from the Caithness. Continuing to fire relentlessly, the trawler's main gun crew do not realise there is a torpedo in the water. The men on the bridge do see the deadly weapon, making its way towards them at high speed. Robert recalls others talking of time standing still as you face an impending catastrophe, and he remembers feeling this as they faced the Heinkel bomber. However, there is something different about this moment of peril as the torpedo is underway and there is a mechanical inevitability to the probable outcome. Men have cast their lots and the outcome is unfolding in front of them and the lack of any influence on the situation makes a big difference to Robert as he feels the seconds tick off one by one as the fast-killing machine tracks its way towards them.

While frozen in this slowed reality, Robert is jolted back to the here and now as a shell hits the E-Boat just in front of its bridge causing a massive explosion. Shocked at the size of the explosion, most likely from onboard torpedoes, no one expects any of the crew to survive as the bridge section is destroyed. Ablaze in seconds, the E-Boat is rendered uncontrollable as it careers towards the right-hand bank of the river over two hundred yards from the trawler. The army is running down the riverbank to search for survivors, but the flames and the risk of another explosion halt them at a safe distance, as they raise their rifles against any signs of life in the water.

Robert returns his gaze to the view ahead of the bow and he is not sure if he can make out the trail of the torpedo. He stares intently at the water and suddenly the signature trail appears in the light from a spotlight on the forward mast. Getting closer he thinks that it is past the point where a premature magnetic detection would have triggered. The blood is pounding in his head as the torpedo closes on them. The weapon is travelling fast and with each terrifying yard of closing distance there is nothing anyone can do. Following its precision managed path, it reaches level with the trawler and passes a few feet away from the hull on the port side, heading past the ship, carrying on to hit the dividing stanchions that separate the flow of the Blyth from the Dunwich River. The explosion shocks everyone and it takes a while to process what has just happened.

The E-Boat continues to burn on the right bank and not a single soul emerges from the fiery wreckage. No one approaches the wreckage for fear of the ordinance exploding and there is a long wait before anyone moves. Manoeuvring the trawler, it moors up against the walled harbour section of the river and many of the crew leave the ship to stretch their legs and recover from what has just happened. They are joined by army officers and naval commanders from Lowestoft and there are many attempts to explain the events of the last few hours. The Skipper is occupied with many discussions and reports, so Robert uses the time to speak to as many of the crew as he can, hopefully getting a feel for how they are coping after the attack. He knows some of the men will not want to talk about it and some will want to go into every fine detail, so he simply gives each man as much time as they need.

Robert cannot understand how the torpedo passed so close to them without the magnetic effect of the ship setting off the trigger. He wonders if this is part of a general problem where the magnetic trigger either goes off prematurely or not at all.

This incident will last long in everyone's memory and for the second time this crew has been attacked by a torpedo and survived.

Chapter 14

The Prize

16th September 1940 – Harwich

Still at the mouth of the River Blyth, Skipper Robinson is working with Army commanders to report on the E-Boat attack. He suddenly collapses. During the engagement, he was hit by a machine gun round at the top of his leg and while the wound is more of a glancing blow, the blood loss is significant. The Skipper receives first aid but he cannot continue on patrol until he has received better treatment and has had time to recover. Following many signals to HQ, the command of the Caithness is transferred to Robert.

At 0800 on Monday morning, Robert is in the wheelhouse of the Caithness and giving orders for the fourth day of their current patrol. Crew allocations are as normal, and Robert is leading, but it is not with his usual team as he must double up on the forenoon watch at the top of their usual patrol sector. The previous day was Robert's first full day in charge, and it passed without incident. Huge waves of enemy bombers are observed flying across the North Sea as the Battle of Britain continues to terrorise the country as the RAF survives in the grip of a fight that is testing the extremes of bravery and endurance.

Making a visit to the wheelhouse from the engine room, Thomas reports that Altman is not fit for duty. Using that as an excuse, he also checks on Robert to see how he is feeling.

'He hit the rum last night and hasn't made his watch this morning.'

'Thank you, Thomas. Where is he now?'

'He's in the forward cabin and I think he's still drunk.'

'Right, I'll deal with him soon. How is everything else?'

'Good, nothing else to report, Skipper.'

'Carry on Thomas,' adds Robert with a smile on his face as he too knows that he is being checked on.

Thomas takes this as a sign that Altman is in for some trouble but also that Robert is taking this in his stride.

'Aye, Skipper,' replies the engineman as he leaves the wheelhouse. Fredricks is at the helm and gives Robert a look that says he also knows what is happening and that word has spread amongst the crew. There is nothing to feel angry about as Thomas is simply looking out for him and Robert appreciates the kindness he is being shown.

Reflecting on Altman's stupidity, Robert is sure it will cost him pay and more importantly the disrespect of his fellow stokers who must pick up the slack.

Signals arrive all morning with details of the Luftwaffe attacks on RAF airfields and the battle that is growing overhead. In the lead up to the anticipated invasion, there are many patrol ship losses as they succumb to mines and aircraft attacks. Identifying so many different risks creates a difficult challenge for those on lookout as they must spot activity in the air and on the sea. Patrol sectors are continually swept for mines, as the patrol vessels respond in kind by protecting the vulnerable minesweepers which have their trawls deployed.

During the morning watch, Robert speaks to as many of the crew as he can. Leaving Altman to last, it allows him to speak to the other crew who had been with him the night before. Very little is said by anyone, so this matter comes down to dealing with just the drunkenness. A brief conversation between Robert and Altman leaves the stoker in no doubt that he has let the crew down. Robert tells him he will not be writing it down in the ship's log and therefore there will be no record of this. Altman appears relieved and accepts the warning, knowing that he has used up any goodwill that he had.

The remainder of the watch is busy but there is little to distract the crew from its normal routine. Robert is relieved as their time on patrol is passing well and he feels the energy he has invested in the men is being returned and is paying dividends. He has spent time with the men, understanding their backgrounds, learning their family situations, and uncovering their concerns. Trust is growing between them all.

Nervously, the patrol continues its work amongst the heightened activity in the North Sea. Robert is again leading at the start of the afternoon watch when Locke indicates there is a signal from Harwich. Reading the details, he immediately tells the helmsman to turn the ship to starboard and head south on a heading of 180 degrees. Asking Slater to stay on lookout, Robert wants to know the minute the patrol's assigned destroyer comes into view. Making his way to the aft cabin, he finds most of the men there and briefs them on the signal, asking them to pass the message to the rest of the crew and to be ready to come to action stations when called. Details in the signal ask them to rendezvous at the Aldeburgh Light Ship, with their current patrol duties taken on by another patrol ship. The Caithness is designated to join the patrol's destroyer, HMS Mentmore, to help with the protection of an E-Boat. The enemy craft suffered a mechanical failure while attacking the destroyer and is now a captured vessel.

Half an hour later, Slater shouts down to Robert on the deck to say that he has sight of the destroyer. Robert orders action stations, transforming the ship to its ready state. Climbing to the wheelhouse he asks Locke to signal to the destroyer to ask for instructions. While waiting for a response, Robert scans the E-Boat through his binoculars and counting the crew standing on its deck, Robert sees the small crew adopting an attitude of surrender. A signal from the destroyer instructs the Caithness to move so the E-Boat is positioned between the two ships, but at a safe distance on both sides. Lowering its launch, the destroyer intends to transport the prisoners from their vessel to scramble nets that have been hung over the side. Once the crew have been transferred, the plan is for the trawler to take the E-Boat under tow and follow the destroyer back to Harwich.

Approaching the craft off their port side Robert takes in all around him. The gun crews are at their stations and respond to the order to cover the enemy vessel in case of a diversionary action or a planned way to launch an attack. Robert concerns himself with the real reason for the E-Boat being stranded as something does not add up for him. Asking for details he receives a signal which shows the destroyer engaged the E-Boat as it came on an attacking run. The destroyer's guns fired on the attacking craft, but the engagement did not develop as the smaller vessel suddenly lost its power and sat helpless in the water. The destroyer's captain chose not to blow the E-Boat out of the water but decided to recover the craft and hand it over to the navy for investigation.

Robert concludes there must be have been a mechanical failure or an electrical fault and he wonders if anyone is intending to inspect the interior. The prize of an intact E-Boat is not lost on Robert and he understands that the Royal Navy will be most interested in the torpedoes onboard as there have been rumours of a new type being deployed. He wonders if the magnetic detonators have been improved.

Having scaled the cargo nets the enemy crew are under the guard of the Royal Navy and Robert is happy they are not bringing prisoners on board the trawler, based on their past experience. Getting a tow line attached is their first problem to solve, followed by the challenge of getting the boat back to Harwich. The E-Boat is shorter than the trawler and a few feet narrower. Trawlers are designed to tow their trawl nets, but an E-Boat is much larger by comparison. However, a naturally buoyant E-Boat is designed to efficiently cut through the water and Robert thinks they have enough power to achieve the tow. Despite favourable sea conditions, his concern is the limited levels of control they will have over the vessel and how to stop it successfully.

Altman and Brown are asked to go to the stern and prepare a towing line from several ropes onboard. The line needs to be secured to bollards and through iron eyes that are found on both sides of the trawler's stern. Robert has asked them to use the longest possible line because he is concerned that if they use too short a length, then the E-Boat will not stop easily, and it will career into the trawler's stern and damage their steering.

Robert has asked Slater to come to the port side of the bridge so he can relay instructions to Stanford on the helm. Reaching the stern, Robert explains to the men there that he intends to back the trawler up so he can climb down to the deck to attach the towing lines. Instructions are passed to Slater on the bridge, where he relays these onto the helm and engine room, allowing them to manoeuvre the trawler to travel astern so it is close to the E-Boat, overlapping its bow. Robert can now be lowered down the short distance onto the deck of the captured craft. Once on the deck, the towing line can be attached to the bow tow post before he returns to the trawler. Slow ahead is the instruction to the engine room as the slack is taken up and the line is checked so it is running freely from the bollards on both sides of the stern. Taking up the tension in the rope, the trawler starts to move slowly through the water and Robert believes the towing arrangement is working, so he decides to stand down from action stations. Being cautious he keeps the two men at the stern to watch over the ropes and the prize trophy they are bringing into port.

The ship sounds and feels different as it ploughs through the water. The engine is working hard to maintain six knots and a strange vibration travels up through the hull to remind everyone of the stress now on the ship. Robert climbs down into the engine room and asks Thomas to join him away from the noise. 'Is this likely to work?'

'Yes, we should be good. We'll maintain a good pressure and watch the revolutions to see how she goes.'

'Have you ever done anything like this before?'

'No, but these ships are very well made, and these steam engines have been running reliably for decades.'

'Don't say that or we'll only get into trouble.'

Thomas laughs and asks, 'what are you really worried about Crawford?'

'It's my first patrol as Skipper and we have this job dropped on us. I know this E-Boat is a great find but perhaps I should have requested another auxiliary ship to help with the tow. Or insisted they use a steam tug out of Harwich.'

'These are difficult things to handle but you are the man in charge and the crew will back you up. They respect you and your experience, so you should stick to your decision until you learn something different.'

'Right, that's good to hear from you. Thank you. One thing I need to know before I head back on deck, what is causing this vibration?'

'The ship's engine and screw are running at the same number of revolutions as they do when we move at ten knots. We're travelling slower with the extra bulk of the E-Boat being pulled through the sea and the vibration is caused by all the extra churn around the screw.'

'We're working just as hard to go slower, right?'

'Yes, that's it.'

'Thank you,' adds Robert as he makes his way to the deck, now feeling more confident in the task he has been given.

With twenty-seven nautical miles to travel, it is now the middle of the afternoon watch and they can only maintain a speed of six knots, just under two-thirds of their normal cruising speed. Robert feels the ship is very vulnerable with the E-Boat in tow and he is also concerned about the light disappearing before they reach port. Robert stays on the bridge and knows he will have to cover the first dog watch because without the Skipper they are short of a watch leader. Sleep has been in short supply this patrol, but he has been able to rely on Harris and Fredricks covering the wheelhouse while he steals some rest or food.

Slater hears the aeroplane long before he sees it and runs around to the port side of the bridge to gain a view. Identification is difficult, but then he spots it as a Junkers JU88 and sticks his head into the wheelhouse to say that a bomber is heading for them. Actions stations are called and the team slot into their positions like clockwork. Robert joins Slater outside and fixes the bomber in his binoculars. The Junkers is a relatively new aeroplane and is regarded as a very fast and versatile addition to the Luftwaffe's collection.

Robert tells the gunners to fire when ready, but as it is coming low and from an angle aft off the port beam, only one Lewis gun can take a shot. Opening fire, the machine gun's tracer shells point a path to the bomber as it approaches, and eventually, the 12-Pounder joins in to unload its shells. Watching for a hit, the crew are disappointed as the speed of the

JU88 is impressive and their attempts to track and fire ahead of the target are currently unsuccessful. The gun crews do not notice that the trawler is not the focus of the bomber. Robert is looking at the broader scene without the aid of binoculars, and he is tracking the bombing run on its intended target, the E-Boat. This is not a chance happening and the attack must have been ordered as the result of some communication from the E-Boat crew before they had to abandon their posts.

The JU88 unloads two bombs from a low level, and both overshoot the towed target. The speed of the bomber is an obvious contributing factor to the miss and the pilot performs a slow turn to enable a slower run. The crew is focusing on the aeroplane and they are blind to the second JU88 that is lining itself up for a run on the E-Boat. Using a more acute angle, this bombing run opens up the area of the vessel's deck to create a larger target. The effective arc of the trawler's machine guns is reduced, and this angle also limits the 12-Pounder, mostly because of its forward position. While the starboard Lewis gun keeps aim and opens fire on the turning bomber, the other guns assess their firing options and switch their aim to the new aeroplane approaching from the east.

The new attacker makes a similar mistake to the first bomber, delaying the decision and releasing its bombs late so they overshoot the E-Boat target. Circling off the starboard side and coming out of their turn, the two bombers start using their forward-facing machine guns to open fire on the trawler. The crew keep up their firing rate in return and the bravery under fire impresses Robert more than anything he has seen from their time together. Based on the strength of the attack, Robert is left in no doubt that the enemy is going to great lengths to stop the E-Boat from spending its days in the hands of the Royal Navy.

Suddenly, he lifts his head as a glorious sound arrives from the west, while the attention on the bridge is focused on the two turning bombers in the east. Swooping low over the bow of the trawler, a Spitfire opens fire with its Browning machine guns on the second of the bombers. Passing in front of them, the Merlin engine sounds gloriously ominous for the enemy.

Locke rushes out onto the bridge with a signal from Harwich answering his original notification of the attack.

'They have scrambled a Spitfire from Martlesham Heath, and that's with all the other air attacks happening in the area,' exclaims Bowes.

'I know,' replies Robert. 'The enemy doesn't want us to have this E-Boat, but some top brass in the navy is very keen for us to keep it.'

Running around the bridge, he shouts to the main gun crew and the machine gunners in turn, to tell them that the Spitfire is attacking the second bomber.

'We need to keep up our fire on the lead bomber. He's starting his run again. Keep firing as we have a better angle now.'

The 12-Pounder launches a salvo of shells at the lead bomber but soon runs out of aiming room as they are in danger of hitting the trawlers superstructure. The starboard Lewis gun is soon in the same situation. Unloading its bombs, the enemy aeroplane draws everyone's view to the stern as the first of two bombs falls into the sea just short of the grey craft, while the second lands in the sea on the other side, causing two plumes of water, both dissected by the E-Boat. Obscured by columns of spray, Robert cannot immediately see the craft to the rear, but his view remains fixed on the stern to see if the tow is still in place. He is relieved when he can see that it is.

'He's got him,' comes the shout from Harris. 'Look the second bomber is going down.'

As they turn to look, the second bomber is ablaze and rapidly losing the little height it had. The impact with the water causes complete destruction of the fuselage and without anyone lingering on the view, their attention moves to the first bomber and the turn it has started off the port side. Climbing and turning quickly, the Spitfire follows a path that takes it over the trawler. Machine gun fire comes from the enemy as the Spitfire is now on an opposing course and the Browning guns deliver their deadly .303 shells to the front of the bomber, instantly killing the gunner in the forward-facing nose section. The pilot is shot in the legs and fights with the controls and the excruciating pain, as another burst from the Spitfire tears through the fuselage, hitting the main fuel tank in the process. Large explosions rip through the aeroplane before it can complete its bomb run. Pulling up sharply, the Spitfire leaves its intercept course and climbs into a cloudless sky. The Caithness crew view this majestic sight and stand rooted to the spot as they respect the destructive power of such an elegant machine. As it returns towards the coast, the Spitfire waggles its wings in a salute to the trawler and some of the crew wave their appreciation in response.

Robert signals that they should continue their journey to Harwich and remain at action stations.

The trawler is making its way to port at a steady speed and the crew remain very much on edge, expecting another airborne attack at any moment. Robert talks to as many of them as he can, passing on his view that the bombers would have known where to find them based on the last signal from the E-Boat crew. He is thinking aloud, and he tells the men it will take the enemy a while to discover the bombers are not returning and an hour will have passed before any other attack is launched. By this time, they will safely be in port.

A signal is sent to the destroyer to ask for closer protection based on the attack, but they have already reached port and have unloaded their cargo of prisoners. With new orders, the destroyer is heading out to sea again to join the original patrol area north of the Aldeburgh Light Ship. Robert feels the priority should be to protect them, but he cannot argue with orders, so he returns to the stern to check on the state of the tow ropes.

Looking over the stern, Robert is not happy with what he finds as the E-Boat is bow heavy and not sitting level in the water. Thinking back to the recent attack, he believes the enemy vessel was hit by machine-gun fire from the bombers and there is a real chance it has developed a serious problem and is taking on water. Robert knows they have a race against time and buoyancy.

Getting close to port, there is the added risk of the E-Boat sinking in one of the channels, blocking all shipping in and out of the vital harbour. He checks the level of the enemy vessel as it ploughs through the light to moderate sea, and he realises there is so much at stake.

As a decreasing amount of the towed boat shows above the water, he decides they must cut her free before it sinks and pulls them under. The vibrations coming through the hull indicate that there is more drag from the E-Boat riding lower in the water and there is little time left for Robert to make the right decision. Running to the wheelhouse, he stops dead in his tracks as he quickly discovers a way to save the enemy vessel and not put the trawler in danger of sinking.

He quickly checks a chart and instructs Fredricks at the helm to turn to port and head due east. Responding to the command the helmsman makes the turn and Robert moves out to the bridge to check the E-Boat's state. It is dropping further in the water and there is a delay as it carries out a turn to follow the direction of the trawler. 'Keep the helm on this course,' shouts Robert as he fetches two of the main gun crew to join him at the stern. Giving instructions, he asks them to watch for his signal from the bridge. When he gives the signal, they are to undo the ropes from the bollards, throw them free from the stern, checking that they cannot fowl the trawler's screw. Once he knows his instructions are clear he returns to the wheelhouse to confirm their position. He knows they recently passed the Shipwash Light Ship on their port side, so he checks their turn to ensure they are heading straight for the Shipwash sandbank.

Robert stands on the bridge with the door to the wheelhouse held open. Trying to look ahead, he wants to see any change in the wave formation or colour of the sea off the bow. Remembering back to the conversations at the Nest with Skipper White, he tries to determine the sea depth and hopefully where the sandbank starts from the colour of the water ahead of them. He detects a change in the sea colour, and he makes his mind up to call for the trawler to slow. He gives the signal to the men at the stern and sees that they are beginning to untie the ropes from their fixings. The ropes have been tightened by the towing tension and they need to lever them apart from the bollards. The ropes are coiled quickly, collected together and thrown clear of the stern. Robert tries to judge the depth ahead, then quickly tells Fredricks to steer hard to starboard and increase the speed to full ahead. The trawler responds as best as it can to this sudden course correction and rolls violently. Robert watches the E-Boat continue on its course straight for the shallower part of the sandbank. The trawler keeps its turn angle and continues to starboard as the enemy vessel runs lower in the water and moves more slowly now that it is not under tow.

After some time of turning in a circle, the trawler comes up right beside the struggling craft. Robert slows the trawler and tries to match the pace of the drifting E-Boat. Seeing a sudden shudder in the enemy craft's structure, he believes the underwater bow has buried itself into the sandbank. It is already low in the water, and they wait and watch as the E-Boat gradually sinks while sitting on the edge of the gradual slope that creates the outline of the sandbank. The plan is working, as the superstructure disappears below the waves and as Robert hopes for this to continue, more of the hull is hidden below the water.

After close to an hour the whole boat has settled on the sandy bottom and it now sits, hidden from view, still easily accessible to Royal Navy salvage divers and recovery ships.

Robert asks Slater to help him pinpoint their position as best they can, before sending a signal to Harwich to explain their situation and provide the location of the prize. He takes a moment to acknowledge the advice he received about the depth of sandbanks and the colour of the water. When he spoke with Skipper White he never thought he would use the skills they talked about in such an audacious way. He now feels more connected to the sea off this Suffolk coast.

It comes to light that there are injuries from the bomber's machine gunfire. Mostly ricochets, these simple flesh wounds are still in need of attention, so a plan is made to overnight in Harwich. There is a relief that wounds can be dressed, and reports can be made describing the operation to recover the E-Boat. Harwich command sends another signal to the Caithness to thank the crew for their efforts to protect the E-Boat and leave it accessible for salvage.

A patrol vessel has been posted to protect the site of the submerged prize and in the light of a new day, salvage crews will find a way to re-float the craft. Robert has heard of something similar done with the wreck of ships close to the harbour. In that case, the salvage crews attached large inflatable floats to the broken ship and used sea tugs to move the sunken ship to a safer location, away from the main harbour entrance. Robert expects the same technique to be used to re-float the enemy craft and bring it to a secure and secret facility.

Robert is satisfied with their efforts and the message of thanks from command is good for the reputation of the Caithness. He has no doubt that some good will come of this, but he must recognise that his role is complete, and he needs to move on. He wonders how the Skipper will react to hearing the news of their exploits and if it will cause any trouble between them. He hopes not, as he has been warming to the Skipper and their conversations have become more important to him. He has had a lot of trust placed in him for the temporary command and Robert believes he has acquitted himself well. Hoping his trust from the Skipper grows, he wants the men to gain confidence in him, so they see him as a future Skipper. He knows he can do the job and thinks there may be an opportunity soon as more trawlers are being requisitioned and they will need crews with their own Skippers. He does not know if he would be assigned to a new ship or if the current Skipper will move on. Robert knows he would prefer to stay with the Caithness crew as he has learnt to work closely with them, and he values their commitment to the service.

Returning to its patrol sector, the Caithness completes a straightforward patrol on Tuesday. Wednesday morning starts with a return to Parkeston Quay and the chance to have an overnight stay ashore. Robert takes the opportunity to write a letter home to ask about the family and to see that all is well. He has hidden the worry he felt during the patrol, but it is causing him to think of all kinds of disastrous outcomes for his family. While on patrol he felt there was one time when he doubted his ability to command, and he was very grateful to have Thomas there to talk to. Surprised by a moment of clarity, he realises that this is the same situation for Skipper Robinson, as in his role as second-hand he is the one person the Skipper can talk to and seek advice from. Understanding his role with more depth he is confident in carrying it out. He realises it is lonelier being a Skipper at war, than when he leads a trawler to fish.

On his way to posting the letter, he searches in two of the pubs to find a newspaper with any news. One of the London daily newspapers carries coverage of the Battle of Britain and the detail is hard to read. Where will this end?

Chapter 15

Patrol Fatigue

19th September 1940, Harwich

A morning at Parkeston Quay is now a very familiar sight for the crew of the Caithness. This Thursday they are heading out for another patrol on their familiar sector north of Aldeburgh Light vessel. Only three days have passed since their celebrated journey with the enemy U-Boat and the full crew is back together now that injuries have healed. Skipper Robinson is back in charge.

The first week of September starts with newspaper and BBC reports full of Battle of Britain stories as the air war is fought in the skies over the east coast. During this time there is a concerted effort by the Luftwaffe to gain air superiority ahead of the planned invasion of the east coast. Earlier phases of the Battle of Britain had seen Luftwaffe bombers attack coastal shipping convoys and ports. The later phases of the battle see bombers directly attack the factories and airfields of the RAF's Fighter Command. The losses inflicted on the RAF are not sustainable and the country becomes more and more set on a course for the inevitable news of mass enemy attacks on the east coast.

In the second week of September, the Blitz starts, and London is still suffering from nightly bombing raids. The bombing of London is a change in strategy for the Luftwaffe, brought about by the RAF bombing Berlin, in retaliation for a stray enemy bomber hitting targets in the City of London. This sequence of events may be the saving of the RAF, as enemy bombers leave airfields and factories alone to focus on London.

The third week of September starts with full newspaper coverage of the vast air battles that take place on Sunday. Wave after wave of bombers are sent to smash London and the southeast, but a resurgent RAF fights a titanic battle in the skies and another crucial day in the war passes with Britain unbroken.

As the fourth week of September arrives, there is still talk of the threat of invasion, and there is little respite from the struggles and fears of families across the country. Patrols continue their repetitive work, and the defence of the nation is upheld.

No one yet knows that Hitler has cancelled his invasion plans.

Yesterday, Robert posted a letter home and is concerned about the flow of letters to the ships, as he has not heard from his family for a while. It is nearly five weeks since he has seen them, and the separation is causing him a vast amount of stress. His letter has some hope included in it as the ship is due for a maintenance overhaul in just over a week's time. As their ship will be out of action for a week, there is probably just one more patrol after this one, before he can make the long journey home for a time of leave. This thought is keeping him going as he misses hearing the sound of his wife and children's voices. He finds faces easier to recollect with the help of photographs but hearing precious voices is harder to recall. Concerning himself with practical matters in his letter, he includes details of his recent wages of £2.14 for the past two weeks. He knows it is vital for his wife to receive this given how costly it is to feed a family at the best of times.

Robert is unaware of the impact his letter will have when it arrives with Alice in a few days' time. He does not know of the recent bomb attack that caused damage to their house and he is not aware of the offer to move into Pembroke to be safe. His letter will give Alice hope as he is due home soon and this seals her decision to remain at home and receive him back into his house when he is on leave.

Following a familiar pattern during the day, the crew wait for the first watch to start at 2000 hours as that normally signals the start of enemy activity in the North Sea. Recently, there are many more E-Boat patrols running as night descends, and this is due to the proximity and number of ports in France and the low countries, used by the enemy. The short distance to the British shipping lanes allows many attacks to be launched and for the boats to easily replenish themselves with ammunition and fuel. Aeroplanes are bombing shipping, and U-Boats are laying an increasing number of mines to disrupt shipping channels. E-Boats are attacking shipping directly but are focusing more on the patrol services and the coastal protection craft that are keeping British shipping safe.

This patrol has five trawlers with the Caithness operating its usual shared northernmost sector. There are many demands on destroyers at this time and as a result, this patrol does not have that welcome protection. The patrol has a combination of four familiar ships and one new trawler, HMT Stowe, crewed by very inexperienced men that have no previous patrol outings to their name. The Caithness is designated HW1 and takes the top half of the northernmost sector. The new trawler takes up the other half of the sector and has the designation HW2. The sector to the south of Stowe is designated HV and is patrolled by the very experienced crew of HMT Highclere, who saw service at Dunkirk. The southernmost ship in the HT sector is HMT Flintshire and as their Skipper is a Lieutenant in the Royal Naval Reserve, he is designated as group officer for the whole patrol.

During the afternoon stages of the patrol, the Caithness and the Stowe meet at the limits of their sectors. Occasionally, they exchange signals to report position and any sightings they have, as Robert and the Skipper are keen to support the new crew on this patrol. The Stowe is the weak link in this chain, but once the Caithness had held that dubious honour and Robert feels like a veteran with three patrols of service to his name.

Robert is asked to join the Skipper in the wardroom and he greets him warmly, 'how are you, Crawford?'

'Very well sir.'

'Good. It's been a while since we have been able to talk, and I want to discuss a few things with you.'

'That sounds bad, sir.'

'No, quite the opposite. It's taken Command at Harwich a little while, but they have given me their report on the recovery of the E-Boat. I know you went through some debriefing after the patrol, but it has taken only a little time to produce the draft report. They need to complete it once they have details of the re-floating and the final move to a secret location. I'll let you read the draft report, but it praises your actions and also recognises your overall command of the patrol. Well done.'

'Thank you, sir. It was a bit risky to do what we did but I'm glad it all went well.'

'Command has recommended that you be given the role of Skipper when the Caithness comes back from its maintenance overhaul in a couple of weeks.'

'That's great news, sir. But what about yourself?'

'Well, this has turned out very well for me as I'm being promoted based on our success. I'll spend some time back at the Nest and then get a new ship and act as group leader for patrols.'

'That is good news.'

'Yes, we've got something to celebrate. We'll have one more patrol together after this one and then some leave before our new assignments.'

'Well done Crawford. You deserve this. I'll miss patrolling with you.'

'Thank you, sir. And the same goes for me.'

A half-moon helps illuminate the calm sea and there is good visibility in the area. Robert is leading the first watch on Saturday, the third day of this patrol. Tracking a large number of aeroplanes in the sky, he observes some at hight and heading for mainland bombing, while others are lower and are attacking shipping in the area. A three-ship minesweeping patrol is clearing mines from around Gap E. While minesweeping, the vessels are close to each other and make good targets for bombers in the area. The auxiliary patrol ships are there to protect the minesweepers and so far no aeroplanes have come close.

Travelling south in sector HW1, Robert spots flashes to the southeast, and a flare, and he believes there are explosions near the minesweepers as they trawl in a north-easterly direction towards the Aldeburgh Lightship. Robert asks Locke to signal the rest of the patrol to pass on his observations. They then turn at the bottom of HW1 and start their journey north. After half an hour they turn again to head south and without explanation, there is a loss of power and the ship slows, telling those in the wheelhouse that there is a problem with the engine.

Making his way quickly to the Engine room, Robert meets Thomas and the two stokers, Ramsey and Altman. It is quieter than normal.

'What's the problem,' asks Robert.

Thomas looks calm and answers, 'We're losing pressure fast. The boiler is fine, but there isn't enough pressure at the inlet to the high-pressure cylinder. I need to check the feed pipes and valves from the boiler, but we can't run the engine while I do that.'

'Fine,' is all that Robert can say at this stage. He knows they are vulnerable as they are drifting. 'I'm going to speak to the Skipper so can you come and find me the minute you know more. I'll be in the wheelhouse or the wardroom.'

The Skipper has made his way to the wheelhouse and meets Robert coming through the doors as the helmsman was directing him to the engine room.

'We've lost engine power, sir. Thomas is looking for the problem. Should we drop anchor?'

'Yes. There is too much activity in this area to be drifting.'

Robert goes directly to the bow himself and cuts the anchor locking mechanism free. The clatter of the chains is not something they hear very often aboard, and the noise does not last long indicating the shallow depth of the water in this area. With the ship no longer drifting he makes his way back to the wheelhouse as he concerns himself with the vulnerability of their position and wants to know what the Skipper intends to do.

'Shall we go to action stations, sir?'

'What have you seen, Crawford?'

'Nothing sir! I'm just concerned we're stopped at the top of our normal patrol and the enemy know our patterns.'

'You're right. Signal action stations and I'll send a signal to the rest of the patrol and the group officer.'

There is an explosion in the distance, and this distracts both the men as they move to the front of the bridge to join Slater who is on lookout. The bell is sounded to call the crew to action stations and the three men try to identify the source of the explosion to the northeast. There are cargo vessels in the main shipping channels, and as it is now dark the low-level bombers are not operating, but there is the constant danger of mines. The mines could easily have been laid from aeroplanes or submarines earlier that day and so the sweeping activities need to continue night and day to keep pace.

Thomas joins the others on the bridge and acknowledges the two senior men. He asks to speak to them both and the manner of his approach serves his purpose as the Skipper asks them to join him below in the wardroom. When the three men are away from the rest of the crew, Thomas gives them his assessment.

'It's not as bad as I'd first thought, sir. We have a leak in the main high-pressure steam feed from the boiler to the engine inlet. It's at a valve where the gasket is gone, so the pipes are fine.'

'What can you do?'

'Well Skipper, I can replace the gasket as we have spare material to cut a new one and we also have a sealing compound I can use. That should fix it.'

'Fine, how long will that take?'

'I can get that fixed in about an hour, sir. But we've taken the heat out of the boiler and I'll have to bring the pressure up slowly to test the new valve seal.'

'So how long before we can get underway?'

'I'd say that will take two hours, sir'.

The following silence tells everyone that they are not in a good place, but they also have little choice. Robert adds, 'I'll go tell the crew what's happening and ensure they keep alert to any attacks.'

'Carry on both.'

'Aye, sir,' comes the simultaneous response as both men leave the wardroom.

'Let me know if you need anything,' Robert adds to Thomas after the door is closed. 'I know the Skipper is not happy, but I'm worried too. You have the experience so take the time you need to do the job right and we'll soon be on our way.'

'Thank you,' are the parting words from Thomas as he appreciates the support from the Second-Hand.

The time passes slowly, and Robert resists the urge to go to the engine room and check on the progress of the repair. Checking the time, he sees it is 2245 hours and they have been anchored for just over an hour now. The night sky is full of high-level bomber squadrons and there are various flashes in the distance that make this the busiest night of any patrol they have had. He continues to watch out for anything that might attack the ship and busies himself between the wheelhouse and checking with the gun crews.

It is 2330 hours when Thomas joins Robert in the wheelhouse. 'I've fixed the valve and tested it up to full running pressure.'

'Well done, Thomas! That's a great job and quicker than you thought.'

'Yes, there weren't any problems, and the new gasket cement makes things easier.'

'Right, I'll tell the Skipper we can get underway.'

Robert speaks with the Skipper and he starts the work to get underway. He stands down the crew from action stations and he makes his move to the bow to weigh the anchor. Operating the steam winch to raise the anchor causes an initial jolt but nothing more. For the second time that night he calls on Thomas to help him solve a mechanical problem, and he also wishes he had not been so hasty to stand the crew down from action stations as he now feels the ship is vulnerable again. Thomas gets his tools and within ten minutes he easily frees up the steam winch, as it was just suffering from lack of use.

The Caithness steams south to continue its normal patrol and reaches the bottom of the HW1 sector just after the start of the middle watch. Robert almost stands to attention on the bridge as he suddenly realises there has been no contact over the telegraph during the past few hours, so he checks with the Skipper, who is now leading the watch. They have a difficult discussion over who will let the patrol know what was happening, but he sees little benefit in continuing that for long. He is more concerned that they have not been in physical or wireless contact with HMT Stowe, and as this is their first patrol he feels duty-bound to look out for them. He agrees with the skipper that they can heave to and wait while he visits Bowes in the wireless room and asks him to send a signal to the Stowe to check all is well. There is no reply after ten minutes so Robert asks the Skipper if they can steam down the HW2 patrol sector to check on the Stowe, and the Skipper agrees.

It is now well into the middle watch as the Caithness is travelling south and is over three miles down the HW2 patrol sector when Harris, the lookout, bangs on the wheelhouse window and points to the dark horizon, as it lights up with tracer fire and what is likely be the firing of a 12-Pounder gun. With their usual speed and efficiency, the crew respond to the call to action stations and are ready to face the enemy, but there is nothing to see apart from the flashes. The only natural conclusion is that the Stowe is coming under attack. The men on the Caithness bridge are focused on the horizon, with their binoculars raised, and their minds set on what they will find a mile ahead of them. Without warning, Slater shouts, 'E-Boat off the port side!'

'Open fire!', shouts the Skipper and the Lewis gun unloads its rounds on the dark shape that is moving fast through the water, making a wake that helps locate it against the dark sea. The 12-Pounder turns but is too late to get a shot away as the boat is close to its maximum speed of forty knots and it disappears as quickly as it arrived.

Those on the bridge try to follow the fast-moving shape, as it circles across their stern, and makes itself visible as it begins opening up with its machine guns. Hitting the superstructure of the Caithness, the E-Boat's bullets make a terrifying sound through the darkness and the crew instinctively duck wherever they stand. As the E-Boat passes down the starboard side, windows in the wheelhouse shatter as the machine gun fire strafes the ship. The Lewis gun is unloading a pan of tracer fire at the E-Boat as it passes, and the 12-Pounder has anticipated its course and turns clockwise to meet it, firing as it starts to turn to port off the bow. The main gun crew are firing at a very high rate while trying to aim ahead of the fast-moving craft. The large shells are not finding their target, but the Lewis gun is having some success as the E-Boat veers away from their fire. The enemy craft speeds southwest and disappears from the sight of the lookouts. Everyone is shaken by the passing attack and the tension is extreme as another could start as suddenly and ferociously as the previous one.

The Skipper and Harris stay on the bridge trying to follow the wake of the E-Boat and guessing on its next possible attack. Robert moves around the ship to check on the crew and to ascertain what damage they have suffered. He is relieved to only find minor injuries from ricochets and flying glass.

Harris shouts down to Robert as he stands next to the main gun crew. 'E-Boat off the port side travelling south.'

Robert shouts back, 'That's not the same boat, it can't be, there must be two of them. Open fire and keep a lookout for the first E-Boat.'

The main gun and Lewis guns start firing on the boat as it moves down the Caithness's port side. There is ferocious fire from the trawler but there is also matching return fire from the enemy that is ripping through the deck area. Brown is lifting a shell for the main gun when he is hit and is instantly killed by enemy fire. The remaining four men on the gun see that there is nothing they can do for their fellow crewman and continue to man and operate the gun as effectively as they can. Despite the loss, there is a determination to blow the E-Boat out of the water in a raw display of revenge. There is nothing Robert can say or do to change the men's approach. Robert stands by the fallen man until he realises the boat is pulling away off the port bow and he must gain height to get a better view.

Climbing the ladder and returning to the bridge, Robert joins the scan for the E-Boat off the port bow. Hearing and seeing nothing, it is not possible to tell where the second boat has gone. Deciding to leave the Skipper and Harris at the front of the bridge,

Robert moves around to the starboard side as he is still concerned about the location of the first boat they encountered. Then, some distance off, and approaching from the northwest, he spots a dark shape cutting through the water. His heart is racing, and he has not felt as fearful as this since starting with the patrol service. His fear is driven by a combination of the limits of the dark and the overwhelming odds against them given the speed, agility and firepower of the multiple craft pitted against them. Comparisons of their situation are stark as they sit on a converted trawler with its poor response, steam engine and its weapons from the Great War. The E-Boats are modern, purpose-built, thoroughbred fighting machines with multiple state of the art marine diesel engines and armaments to match. This is not a fair fight between equals.

In a moment of lucid tranquillity, Robert remembers the cause he joined and the price it might demand. His family comes into clear focus and he believes they will not understand the choices he has made.

The first boat has circled around from the south and is now approaching the Caithness broad on the starboard quarter. Training his eyes on the craft he sees another shape launch into the water and it is heading fast and straight towards him. He moves quickly to warn the others, but there is no time, as a massive explosion rips the ship apart.

Chapter 16

The Enquiry

25th September 1940, Great Eastern Hotel, Harwich

Commander Wilkes is sitting at the head of the table set out for the leaders of the Royal Navy Board of Enquiry. Inviting everyone present to take their seats, he addresses them with his opening remarks.

'Welcome to this Board of Enquiry into the sinking and loss of all hands of HMT Caithness. Today, I am joined by Lieutenant Dickerson and Lieutenant Williams who will be helping to conduct this enquiry. First, we start with the witnesses.'

Lieutenant Williams stands and invites Commander John Davidson, R.N. to make his way to the small table and chair set aside for those presenting evidence.

'Are you Commander John Davidson, R.N., Senior Officer, Auxiliary Patrol, Harwich?

'Yes.'

'Please can you tell us of the events of the night of 21st September 1940, regarding HMT Caithness and HMT Stowe?'

'Yes. The patrol pattern followed a recent change that had been made and the Caithness and Stowe were sharing a patrol sector at the northern limit of the Harwich section of the coast, designated

HW. We have sightings and signals that show the two vessels on patrol between the Aldeburgh Lightship and a position to the east of Dunwich. I have transcripts of the signals sent during the 22nd September.'

'Thank you, Commander. Do you have anything to add based on enquiries to Lowestoft or Yarmouth?'

'No, nothing to report.'

'Thank you, Commander. You may return to your seat,' invites the Lieutenant.

The enquiry continues with two witnesses from HMT Stowe and the Group Officer for the patrol from HMT Flintshire. The Stowe witnesses explain their sightings through the evening and night, covering details of their wireless problems and how they came under attack after midnight by two E-Boats. The group officer gives evidence of his observations during the patrol and how he sent HMT Highclere to the north of their normal patrol to search for the cause of tracer fire and explosions. The Highclere meeting with the Stowe is confirmed and the evidence they gave is verified.

There was a detailed discussion about contact with the Caithness and when she was assumed missing. It was Sunday 22nd September at 1100 hours when the search for the Caithness was started and this continued until 2000 hours when identifiable wreckage was found. There were items found that included a ship's Carley Float, a hammock and a kit bag with the name Altman, a HMT Caithness crew member, inked on it.

With all the evidence collected the Board of Enquiry adjourns so it can make its recommendation. The findings of the enquiry were sent to the Flag officer In Charge, Harwich the following day 26th September 1940. The report concluded that HMT Caithness was probably torpedoed by an E-Boat at 52 degrees 14 minutes north on its patrol course between Aldeburgh and Dunwich.

Various recommendations are made to improve the operation of patrols following this attack. The practice of "heaving to" is to be discouraged and the long distances between different patrol vessels can create gaps for the enemy to exploit. Based on the evidence given it is clear that E-Boat crews are very familiar with the patrol layout for trawlers, so they should vary their speed and take on a zig-zag course where possible. The findings also highlight the need for better training and practise facilities for main gun crews. The final recommendation suggests the better deployment of destroyers to support patrols and the specific role given to a senior officer onboard to coordinate better communications with the patrol vessels.

The findings conclude that while improvements could be made to operating procedures it is a pity these could not have been done before, and in the meanwhile valuable lives have been lost.

The Enquiry findings are marked "Classified", and the file is set closed to public viewing until the year 2041. Families of the crew will not learn of the circumstances of the deaths of their loved ones for many years to come.

It is Saturday 28th September 1940, when Alice receives a telegram. As she starts to read she cannot get past the words, 'I regret to inform you …' She crumples on the floor and remains there for some time, unable to face the prospect of life without her beloved Robert. The day suddenly has no meaning, and she does not know what to do next. The telegram goes on to say that Robert has been lost at sea and is presumed dead. The word "presumed" taking on a ghastly meaning as it hints at the smallest amount of hope in what is a hopeless situation.

She picks herself up and walks to the kitchen where the children are eating breakfast. Their lives are about to change so dramatically but she cannot find a way to tell them yet. They are so young. She vows to be strong and help them survive this life-changing ordeal. Three children will grow up without a father and Alice is devastated to think how they will cope. How will the boys turn out as men without his influence? How will a daughter feel without his dependability?

Alice's sister is on hand to help with the children over the coming days but there does not seem to be a break in the grief as there is no funeral or burial to attend. There is no way to say goodbye and there is no opportunity to gather and remember the life of someone so important to the wider family.

In the coming weeks, the house becomes a huge empty place that cannot be filled with even the slightest sound of joy from the children playing. Alice is concerned about how she will afford to live there on a war widows' pension and there is increased danger from more regular bombing raids close to the dockyard. These factors all contribute to Alice's decision to move the family away from the town. Without Robert, this is no longer their home.

With her family's help, she manages to find a house in an idyllic location close to the beach at Freshwater East. The children love their new house as it is peaceful and quiet in comparison to the house in the town. There are fantastic places for the children to play in the dunes behind the beach and there is a sandy shoreline and water to explore with their mother.

Alice remembers it as a place where she once felt so happy. The family time on the beach with Robert a few months ago is more than a treasured memory. It is the essence of Robert as a family man, and it acts as a place of remembrance by the sea that was such a great part of his life.

Historical Note

I wanted to tell the story of a little-known part of the protection provided to Britain in the early stages of World War Two. The story started from family research and a Commonwealth War Graves entry for my paternal Grandfather. I knew that my Grandfather had been killed in the war, but it took a reasonable amount of research to piece together his story from historical records and the reminiscences of family members. The key idea for this story came when I was given a copy of an Admiralty Board of Enquiry report, for the loss of HMT Loch Inver on 21st September 1940. This ship was lost with all hands and one of those who made the ultimate sacrifice was my Grandfather, Peter Ritchie Strachan, Second-Hand, Royal Naval Patrol Service, LT/JX 215886.

The book's character of Robert Crawford was inspired by Peter, but all other characters are completely fictional and bear no relation to anyone living or dead. To be able to tell the story I have had to invent day to day details of home life and invent a narrative for the time in the RNPS and during the sea patrols.

From a family perspective, I have used broad details, including the beginnings in Fraserburgh, the move to Milford, meeting his wife at The George Hotel, the start of the family in Pembroke and the move to Pembroke Dock. Some themes in the story such as the Oil Tank Fire, the loss of the Caithness and the Board of Enquiry are inspired by real events.

The chapters covering training, all patrols at sea, the second bombing of Pembroke Dock, the events at Parkeston Quay, rescuing the crew of a minesweeper, shooting down a bomber, the Blyth River raid and the capture of the E-Boat are all fictitious and are not intended to have any connections to real events.

I have invented the names for all ships in the story, but I do want to mark the terrible loss of life and the great sacrifice made by many at this time. Life in the RNPS must have been very hard and those who served must have experienced moments of sheer terror.

I wish I had been able to speak to my Grandfather and hear of his life at sea. I had the pleasure to meet his brother on a few occasions including one where we explored the harbour area in Fraserburgh. I have a copy of the last letter my Grandfather sent to his family and it is dated 18th September 1940. I have represented the contents of the letter and I feel the strains and exasperation of a man who wanted to see his family so much but was denied the chance.

The locations for family events such as the houses and the George Hotel are inspired by real locations, including the move to Freshwater East following the loss of my Grandfather. I remember my father taking me to the beach when I was young, and I wish I had understood the significance for him during the times we spent there. The story also references the Oil Tank fire, and this features heavily in my family history as my maternal Grandfather was a fireman from Pembroke Dock who fought the blaze.

The thoughts and emotions expressed in some parts of the book are autobiographical. If there are any historical mistakes, then I offer my apologies.

Acknowledgements

I would like to thank Nicki, my wife, for her valuable feedback on the early versions of this book. Nicki was an excellent source of proofreading but also a willing sounding board for ideas and connections.

I would like to thank my children, Huw, Rhiannon and Ioan for their interest in the project and their comments on sections of the book. In the main, this book was written for them, so their generation can remember.

I am thankful to Sarah and Ian Strachan for their original sources of family history but also for giving me a copy of the Admiralty Board of Enquiry.

I am also grateful for the support and encouragement given by Jo O'Dwyer.

Catrin Hughes helped enormously with an early review of draft chapters and with her insights into creative writing.

Ray Pentland gave generously of his time by reading an early draft and providing insight into the Battle of Britain timelines. Thank you.

I thank Glenda Kennett for the details of how my Grandparents first met.

I thank Richard Collard for his excellent feedback and the broader discussions on the content of the story.

I thank Phil White for his excellent feedback and his keen eye for mistakes.

Bibliography

The document that started it all is the original Royal Navy Board of Enquiry document that covers the loss of trawler that my grandfather served on:

National Archives ADM 1/10786 - HM SHIPS - DAMAGE AND LOSS (31): Loss of HM Trawler LOCH INVER: Board of Enquiry [Contains public sector information licensed under the Open Government Licence v3.0.].

I also researched his service records, and they were provided by Naval Command Records in Portsmouth: JX215886 Record of Service, Discharged Dead Rating Cards and Medal Entitlement Card.

I had visited the museum of the Royal Naval Patrol Service Association some years ago when travelling to the Lowestoft Naval Memorial. Viewing the Associations web site is a way to see how the RNPS history is kept alive {www.rnpsa.co.uk}.

For details of the Lowestoft Naval Memorial and the work done by the Commonwealth War Graves Commission visit {www.cwgc.org}.

Printed in Great Britain
by Amazon